Likely Story: Red Carpet Riot

Likely Story:

Red Carpet Riot

David Van Etten

Alfred A. Knopf

New York

THIS IS A BORZOI BOOK PUBLISHED BY ALFRED A. KNOPF

Visit us on the Web! www.randomhouse.com/teens

Educators and librarians, for a variety of teaching tools, visit us at www.randomhouse.com/teachers

Library of Congress Cataloging-in-Publication Data
Van Etten, David.
Likely story : red carpet riot / David Van Etten. — 1st ed.
    p. cm.
Summary: Sixteen-year-old Mallory, daughter of a soap opera star, is faced with new challenges when the soap opera that she created and wrote is nominated for an Emmy Award and she has to deal with sneaky saboteurs while trying to decide between her boyfriend and her show's leading man.
ISBN 978-0-375-84680-9 (trade)—ISBN 978-0-375-94680-6 (lib. bdg.)—
ISBN 978-0-375-85356-2 (e-book)
[1. Television—Production and direction—Fiction. 2. Soap operas—Fiction.
3. Interpersonal relations—Fiction. 4. Self-perception—Fiction. 5. Mothers and daughters—Fiction. 6. Emmy Awards—Fiction. 7. Hollywood (Los Angeles, Calif.)—Fiction.] I. Title. II. Title: Red carpet riot.
PZ7.V2746Lir 2009
[Fic]—dc22
2008050858

The text of this book is set in 13-point Galena.

Printed in the United States of America
June 2009
10 9 8 7 6 5 4 3 2 1

First Edition

prologue

I was just four years old when I saw my mother die her first death.

She'd gone undercover at a chocolate convention to sniff out the lunatic who'd snuffed out her *Hoopla* magazine colleague, food critic Lionel Lumley. The paramedics said it was the result of an accidental overdose of artificial sweetener, but my mother didn't buy it. She had little use for medical professionals of any kind, having twice woken up mid-operation, the victim of botched anesthesia—once to find her neurosurgeon cavorting with a nubile nurse and once as a surgical team was prepping to harvest her organs for sale to an ailing dictator from the South American nation of "Perugentina."

She hadn't meant to go undercover on her own. She'd gone shoulder to shoulder pad with Bret Beauregard, Shadow Canyon's police commissioner and punching bag, insisting that Lionel Lumley would have tasted the difference between pure and processed sugar at twenty paces—*upwind*. "No way would he be undone by a spoonful of Sweet'n Low!" she insisted. "This was foul play!"

Bret appreciated Mom's loyalty to her friend, but explained that the law didn't recognize women's intuition as grounds for opening an investigation. His hands were tied, but he knew Mom's weren't. He warned her not to do anything nutty. . . .

"Like look into it myself?" she asked. Hitting him with her trademark dramatic lean-in/arched-eyebrow combo, she added, "I didn't spend two weeks in night school to get my PI license for nothing, Commish."

The trail of tasty evidence finally led her to the back rooms of the Shadow Canyon Candy Convention. There she discovered a cabal of evil pastry chefs plotting to make all of Shadow Canyon addicted to their designer sugar substitute (called Devil Dust).

Caught in the act eavesdropping on a conversation in which the cabal revealed the full extent of its plans, Mom was bound and gagged and suspended over a vat of molten fudge, into which she was slowly lowered. As she was swallowed up in goo, the head goon, a pear-shaped Frenchman by the name of Henri, offered this solace: "Worry not, *ma petite sucrerie.* Your Death By Chocolate will be zee toast of zee town."

I saw the whole thing happen . . . and did nothing.

Not that I was in a position to do anything. I wasn't hiding inside a walk-in freezer, waiting for the right moment to fish her out. I was home. On the couch. Watching my mother drown in ice cream topping on network TV.

Still, I tried. I desperately hit the buttons of the universal remote, looking for that universally remote chance of saving her. But the power of Panasonic couldn't change her fate. She was lost to a chocolatey grave . . .

Until she walked through the front door two hours later.

Back then, my day-to-day rearing was mostly the responsibility of a bunch of nannies for whom I had little patience. They preferred popping bonbons to reading stories and were content to farm me off to the tender loving care of the TV. This was fine by me: The only attention I craved was my mother's, and the only exposure to her I could always count on was *Good As Gold*'s three o'clock time slot. I was young enough and alone enough to take what I could get . . . even if it messed with my head. I was a preschooler, as impressionable as a piece of unchewed gum, getting my strongest dose of family from a soap opera. Naturally I began to think of Mom as her character, Geneva, and Geneva as Mom. It didn't help matters that she had a habit of bringing her work home with her. One afternoon I watched Geneva/Mom tryst with Shadow Canyon's perpetually shirtless dogcatcher. That night Mom/Geneva brought him home to "run lines" . . . in the hot tub.

So her arrival in the living room on the day of her demise threw me for a loop-de-loop. I flung my arms around her legs and cried, vowing never to eat a Hershey bar again.

"Mallory, darling, you do know that what you see on TV isn't real, don't you?"

Still to this day, I don't know whether she was disturbed by my fear or annoyed by my stupidity—she regularly told me to stop being childish, even when I was four.

I gave her the nod she obviously expected, but she could tell I remained unconvinced. She took it more as a compliment to her acting ability than as a comment on her mothering. "I did give a good performance, didn't I?" she said, wriggling

5

from my embrace. She had no time to suffer my confusion—the People's Choice Awards were mere hours away. She'd brought home half her *GAG* wardrobe (all gowns) and had contracted her trusted makeup artist, Gina, to do her up for the occasion. Never mind that the People hadn't actually chosen her for anything. If a red carpet was unrolled within a hundred-mile radius of Los Angeles, my mother was on it. She whisked upstairs to begin preparations, but Gina, always better tuned to my emotions, hung back and sat me down.

"You want to know something?" she said, her voice as friendly as a rainbow. "I was pretty bothered by your mom's chocolate soak, too."

"You were?" I sniffled.

"Uh-huh. Think about it. They filled that tub with a *ton* of good chocolate! Chocolate that belonged on sundaes and in cookies and cakes. But mostly," she confided, "in my belly."

"No one could eat that much chocolate," I declared.

"I bet the two of us could." And just like that, Gina had coaxed a smile out of me. This was her easy talent, and I loved her for it.

Gina must have said something to Mom, because the next day I was allowed on the set for the first time since I was a baby. They figured if I saw the show being made, I'd know it wasn't real.

I learned very quickly that Geneva's adventures came courtesy of a pack of jaundiced, chain-smoking writers; that the sets were as tough as wet cardboard; and that she who controlled the snack table controlled the world. The most important lesson I learned, though, was that my mother and Geneva were not the same person.

A few hours in, Gina sent me over to the studio floor with a delivery of fresh blotting powder for the actors on set. Taping was in progress, so I tiptoed to an out-of-the-way spot behind the boom operators and waited for the stage manager to call "Cut." The scene was Geneva's office. My mother stood opposite Jim Owens, the actor who played her worrywart lawyer, Snap.

                    SNAP
          Take the plea deal, Geneva.

                   GENEVA
          And let them brand me an eco-
          terrorist? Not on your life.

                    SNAP
          If they get a conviction,
                you'll hang.

                   GENEVA
          What if it was you, Snap?
          What if you were the one
             wrongfully accused of
             murdering all those
                 chinchillas?

                    SNAP
          We're talking about your
          life, Geneva. And more than
          that, we're talking about
                your future.

GENEVA

No, we're talking about my
good name. And that's worth
something—not just to me but
to the readers of *Hoopla*. I
won't have them believing the
worst of me. I won't give in.
I can't. Please, Snap. Fight
for me. (SHE DISSOLVES IN
TEARS AND

"Cut!" Shoulders sagged across the room, and the camera-men muttered curses. Mom flagged down the stage manager, pissed.

"That was the sixth take already. What's wrong now?" she wanted to know.

The director emerged from the control room, waving a script. "I'll tell you what's wrong. The script calls for Geneva to DISSOLVE IN TEARS, but I'm not seeing any waterworks."

"We've been over this, Bob. Geneva would not cry in this situation. She's made of steel. Raw iron steel."

"She's been charged with a capital crime, honey. I don't care if she's the Eiffel Tower, she's going to have a moment of vulnerability."

Mom rolled her eyes. "Geneva doesn't 'do' vulnerable."

"Or do you just not know *how* to do vulnerable?" Bob shot back.

Jim gasped. All eyes targeted my mother. Had anyone ever had the nerve to accuse my mother of being less than a con-summate thespian?

No one spoke. No one moved.

My mother blinked.

My mother, who never blinked.

Bob held her stare a moment longer, wondering if he'd caught a tiger by the tail. He opened his mouth to backtrack, but my mother silenced him with a sweep of her hand and instructed the stage manager to roll tape. The crew resumed positions, Bob scurried back to the control room, and the stage manager gave my mother the go-ahead.

GENEVA

No, we're talking about my good name. And that's worth something—not just to me but to the readers of *Hoopla*. I won't have them believing that I am the worst that there is. I am not a killer of chinchillas! I love chinchillas. As a little girl, I— (SHE BEGINS TO CHOKE UP) I had a chinchilla named (A SINGLE TEAR FALLS DOWN HER CHEEK) Checkers! So if not for me, or my readers, then for Checkers. I won't give in. I can't. Please, Snap. Fight for me. Fight for— Checkers. (SHE DISSOLVES IN TEARS AND CRUMBLES TO HER

KNEES. SNAP TAKES HER IN HIS
ARMS AND COMFORTS HER. FADE)

The scene ended, and the crew was ordered to take five, but not before Jim proclaimed, "Now *that* was acting." My mother's performance was over as abruptly as it had begun. Her face betrayed no sign of the tears that had dangled there moments ago. She was, once again, the tough-as-nails Mom/ Geneva I'd known her to be. She stormed off to the control room to put Bob in his place, unaware I'd witnessed the whole thing. Unaware that, just then, I'd seen her die again. Or at least disappear.

It wouldn't be the last time.

"I don't know how it's done in New York, but here in Hollywood, no one likes anyone."

one

My friend Scooter has a pretty typical after-school job stocking shelves at Store-Mart. His boss meets him at the door every Tuesday, Thursday, and Sunday at four, usually with a mop and good news along the lines of "cleanup in aisle three." On his way to the pukepile, a co-worker begs Scooter to please-pleaseplease take her Friday night shift so she can go out with her boyfriend 'cuz it's their forty-six-hour anniversary! And then he's run down by a gang of irate customers waving their nubby fingers in his face, demanding to know why their favorite press-on nails were discontinued.

I've got a job, too. Like Scooter's, mine comes complete with angry mobs and needy colleagues. My boss also delights in meeting me at the door with talk of disaster. Only he never carries a mop.

"Break out the red pen, Mal. You have to change Harry and Carmen's scene so it no longer includes the banana splits," he said to me now, plucking a piece of lint from my shoulder.

Eight a.m. and I was sighing already. "Today is not the day, Richard. You're the executive producer, so make an executive decision for once. Replace the ice cream with frozen yogurt. I'm not rewriting three pages of dialogue because a couple of actors are deathly afraid of cardio."

"The problem," Richard informed me, "is not that Wardrobe is out of elastic waistbands. If you bothered to read the memos from our friends at Standards and Practices, like any responsible head writer, you'd know that *banana* has been added to their list of objectionable words and phrases. Apparently you can no longer say *banana* in daytime."

"Are you kidding? What do the network censors have against fruit?"

But Richard was off and running mid-sentence before I'd even finished my question: ". . . story meeting tomorrow, at which I hope you will finally reveal the identity of the killer of the student council president."

"Hey, it wasn't my idea to jump-start the show with the murder of a character no one knew and no one cared about," I reminded him.

He rolled right over me. "Plus I need three ideas for integrating soap products into a front-burner story. A poisoned loofah or an incendiary bath bomb, something like that. Don't think too hard about it."

"Why don't you save us both a migraine and do the thinking for me, Richard?"

"Believe me, I'm considering it."

He smiled when he said it, as if to prove to passersby that all was well. Nothing to see here, just a couple of friendly creative-types having a warm chat. But the grin was a thin veneer for solid ice underneath.

"What's the matter, boss? Wake up on the wrong side of the bed?"

He didn't bother to contradict me. I'd scored, but he'd sooner give up his Amex Black than admit it.

Richard slung an arm over my shoulders, walking me through security. "I know things have been tense between us lately, Mallory."

This might've been because he was sleeping with one of the stars of our show . . .

"And here I thought I was imagining it."

. . . who happened to be my mother.

"You're stressed. I'm not surprised, with all the buzz."

Buzz. Swarm. Bees. Kill.

"You've always got a finger on the pulse, Richard."

And on my mother.

"You're not the only one with anxiety, Mallory. The cast made off with half my stash of Xanax by seven. But as much as I care about their well-being during this trying time, I know yours is the hand that most needs holding."

If you try to hold my hand, I thought, *I will break all your fingers.*

"Richard, so far I have heard nothing that you couldn't have put into an e-mail."

I'd actually trusted him. Even when he was giving me a hard time. Little did I know he'd been auditioning to become my mother's new husband.

"But then we wouldn't have had this valuable face time."

Her *fourth* husband.

He thrust the offending scene into my hand and gave me

his Lawgiver look. "Quit it with the amateur attempts to sabotage me with the network. They may give me a talking-to for letting these double entendres nearly get through to tape, but believe me, they know exactly who wrote them."

Scowling on the inside, sweetness on the out, I asked, "Anything else?"

"Be nice to your mother."

I thought he was kidding. "Why don't I just ride my unicorn over to Shangri-la and pick you a bouquet of four-leaf clovers while I'm at it?"

He wasn't kidding. "She could use your support right now."

"She could also use a chemical peel, but you didn't hear it from me."

Still not kidding.

I sighed. "What do you want from me, Richard?" I asked. "We've always lived by the Golden Rule at our house. I do unto Mom as I would have her do unto me. Which is to say: Nothing is done or un-done to anyone at all. That's how it's always worked."

"*Has* it worked, Mallory?"

Richard had clearly been to his shrink that morning.

"The two of you are a True Hollywood Story waiting to happen," he cautioned.

"And I have no doubt you'll be ready and waiting to produce the hell out of it. Please steer clear of my relationship with my mother. If I find out that you've booked us on *Oprah* to kick-start the healing, there won't be a toupee maker alive able to re-sod your scalp."

Apparently Richard didn't mind playing fast and loose with

his coif. "I'm going to do whatever it takes to get you two right again."

"Whatever it takes? I admire your *research methods*. And that, Richard, was a double entendre."

"I do care about you, Mallory. I want you to be happy."

As evidence, he flagged down a passing intern and instructed him to "fetch" me a latte. This was what I dealt with on a daily basis: a boss whose vocabulary suggested feudal Europe, not feuding Hollywood. "You'll feel better with a little steamed soy milk in you. I can't have my wunderkind off her game on such a big occasion."

I protested, but not because I didn't crave the coffee and not even because the intern was actually six years older than me. Soon after *Likely Story* got the green light, I confessed to my mother my unease at having a hundred seasoned professionals reporting to me, a high school student. Mom didn't bother to look up from her *Marie Claire*. "You were born in LA," she droned. "Being catered to is in your genes." I got over giving orders pretty quickly.

But there was that other, much more important reason I had to nip Richard's patronizing in its ever-growing bud. "A five-dollar coffee isn't going to buy the peace, Mr. Boss Man."

He overrode my veto and sauntered off toward the control room. "Be sure to be home for dinner tonight. We're ordering Indian."

I had to break off their engagement. Right away.

"Look at you, you're all nervous."
That voice. Like the sound of Christmas presents
unwrapping.

two

I retreated to the writers' room, which for me was kind of like going to the area in the high school cafeteria where you know that no one will make fun of what you're wearing or anything you say.

My faithful friend (and staff writer) Tamika was waiting for me.

"I hear bananas are verboten," she said.

"Yup. No doubt cherries will be next."

"And cantaloupes."

"And pears."

Tamika nodded with mock seriousness. "Clearly, all fruit is out."

"At least Richard had to get yelled at by Standards and Practices. He had the look of someone who'd just had his wrist slapped raw. But he also had the look of someone who *liked* it."

"Maybe that's enough. Maybe that will finally teach him to back off your mom and not to mess with you," Tamika said.

Oh, how I wished. "Or it'll teach him to read the scripts more carefully before releasing them to the wide world. I think if we're going to get Richard to break off the engagement, we need to do more than cram a scene full of sight gags requiring lots of melons and a cucumber."

Tamika mulled this over. "So we move on to Plan B."

"Oh, good."

Silence.

"Uh . . . tell me, Tamika. What's Plan B?"

"This is your show, girl. I'm just along for the ride."

We came up with the following list:

• Discover Richard is embezzling from the show. Blackmail ensues.

• Discover Richard has been smuggling blood diamonds. Blackmail ensues.

• Discover Richard has been imprisoning his good twin in an (a) attic, (b) meat locker, (c) wishing well, (d) coffin, (e) bank vault, (f) ship's hold, (g) cargo container, (h) car trunk, (i) abandoned mine shaft, (j) abandoned sauna, (k) deserted island, (l) ghost town, (m) haunted house, (n) haunted hayride, (o) corn maze, (p) catacomb, (q) Underground Railroad tunnel, (r) underwater grotto, or (s) lobster trap. Blackmail ensues.

• Discover Richard is a woman. Blackmail ensues.

• Discover Richard is a man. Blackmail ensues.

"The trouble with blackmail," I said, yawning, "is that it's illegal. And the last time we tried to trap Richard, I was arrested."

"But he dropped the charges," argued Tamika.

"And then threatened to leak the whole thing to TMZ! So

I'd prefer to avoid any more legal entanglements, thank you. I've seen enough bars to last me 'til my twenty-first birthday."

Tamika bit her lip. Which was Tamika for *You're not gonna like this, but . . .*

"What?" I asked.

Her attempt to shrug off my question was just for show.

"There is one way to put the brakes on your mom's marriage plans, and you can do it without the fuss and muss of plotting and scheming. It's kind of out-there, though."

"Don't make me get out the pliers, Tamika."

"You could tell her how you feel about it."

"Going back to the blackmail idea . . . ," I said.

"Would it be that big a deal to have a heart-to-heart with your mother?"

"That scenario requires two hearts, I believe."

Tamika waved me off. "You're too harsh."

"I told you how I reacted when they broke the engagement news to me, right?"

"You fainted."

"My head hit the floor. Have you been in our study? I missed the Oriental rug by three inches and smacked the marble floor instead. I still have the wound." I swiped back my hair, exposing the scar. "If four stitches didn't get my mother's attention, no meeting of the minds will, either."

Not even Tamika could argue with that. Or maybe she just knew not to push it. I wished I did.

"Why should I be the one to take the first step?" I blurted. "Why should I put myself out there and tell her I want to fix things? Why can't she want to fix things with me? All my life I was just a speed bump to my mother, something to slow down for, something that ruined her ride. Then *Likely Story* comes along, and suddenly I'm no longer an obstacle—now I'm her chauffeured ride to success! And not only is she driving all over me, she's giving Richard a ride, too. She nearly stole the show. He nearly ruined it. Put them together and I shudder to think what'll become of it."

Still, Tamika needed confirmation. "So no good would come of telling her this?"

I was ninety-five percent sure such a conversation would only aggravate my ulcer. Ninety-five percent sure it would only lower my expectations of my mother . . . right through the floor. Ninety-five percent sure I'd get emotional, ninety-five percent sure she'd turn it around on me.

But that left five percent. Five percent that remembered my mother could, indeed, *cry*. Five percent that knew she was capable of emotion.

Five percent that wasn't sure of anything.

Luckily, the rest of the writers soon arrived, and we resumed wrestling over how to fold the element of Ryan's worsening drug problem deeper into Jacqueline's family crisis without leaving Sarah, our presumptive heroine, out of a storyline. We hadn't even begun to climb out of the murder mystery hole into which we'd dug ourselves. It was a tricky situation, and I didn't want to leave them to figure it out on their own.

About fifteen minutes later, Richard slipped in. We'd long since given up on Ryan and were comparing our stripper names instead (first pet's name + street on which one grows up = Rufus Castle, Fergie Red Post, Matches Peppercorn, Max

Wellington, to name a few). Richard could see we were getting a lot of valuable work done.

Before I knew what was going on, Richard was saying it was time for me to go, and was hustling me toward an idling Suburban.

"Don't forget to smile," he said. "And if she doesn't get a nod, you'll need to do damage control right away."

I almost laughed. I knew the drill better than he did.

Richard may have spent the night with my mom, but he'd never been with her on the day the Daytime Emmy nominations were announced.

That job was mine.

And we were about to do it on live TV.

Perhaps Alexis did indeed have a heart where I'd previously envisioned a breeding ball of snakes.

three

"I want him naked," said the director. "As naked as possible."

Mom always said the liveliest conversation in Hollywood was found not at The Ivy and certainly not in a room full of writers. There is a place where Nobel Prize–winning plastic surgeons, shark-attack victims, and Disney Channel stars sit down to compare notes . . . and that place is the makeup room of an afternoon talk show, where all brows—high, middle, and low—converge into one big, unsightly uni. *Blabbermouth*'s makeup room was no exception.

The show's director jabbed a finger at his frightened costume designer. "Give me flesh. The more the better." By and large the rule in show business is to *clothe* actors; the exception to that rule appeared to be *Likely Story*'s male star, Dallas Grant.

The costumer dogged her boss the length of the room.

"Look, Cynthia, I'm not asking for an obscenity charge. I just want some skin. This kid Dallas drives *Likely Story*'s ratings, so we might as well have his pecs drive our nomination ceremony. Bargain with him. Offer him a sock and work from there, okay? But hold the line at shirtless. And tell him it's a 'brave' choice. Actors always fall for that."

Ha, I thought. There was no way Dallas was going to fall for that.

Not my Dallas.

Who wasn't mine, really.

I mean, at all.

"It's not going to happen," I told Cynthia once her boss was gone.

Cynthia couldn't believe it. "Why? He's got more abs than an Olympic swim team. He must be dying to flaunt 'em."

True about the abs, but false about the flaunting.

"What's the story with him and Francesca?" my makeup artist asked, taking aim with an eyeliner pencil. "They're so hot on screen. Are they dating in real life, too?"

"No, thank God!" I exclaimed. God? Smooth move, Mallory. Beneath the MAC, I was blushing a three-alarm blaze.

"You know how it is," I spun. "Two leads hooking up sounds good on paper, makes for buzz and some punch in the ratings. But then there's the inevitable break up and make up and break up again, followed by temper tantrums and thrown chairs. All of which is hilarious for reporters but total purgatory for anyone else on the set."

"Is Dallas the type to hissy-fit, though? I mean, you work with him. . . . What's he really like?"

Teen Vogue, Defamer, and *Soap Opera Digest* had all endeavored to solve that riddle. "Breathes life back into soaps," wrote *SOD. Teen Vogue* called him "a witchy brew of Jake Gyllenhaal's sensitivity, Ryan Phillippe's focus, and Johnny Depp's charisma . . . only *much* younger." *Defamer* was a tad less circumspect. "Inspires feminists everywhere to show up at his door bearing homemade baked goods," it proclaimed.

Nobody had it exactly right.

Sure, he deserved to crack *People*'s Sexiest Men Alive top ten. Damn straight, *TV Guide,* his acting was nothing short of "inspiring." And who was going to question *Dog Fancy*'s claim that he doted on his pug, Muggles?

But where were the quotes about his loyalty or his friendship? About that effect he had—it could be the most awful, rainy, deadly Monday morning, and you could be waking up to the worst song ever on your alarm, and just the thought that you were going to see him suddenly made it worth getting out of bed. Was there a word for that? I wanted to invent one, but the best I could come up with was *Dallas*.

I might've done the gushing myself—if I were his publicist. Or his agent. Or his girlfriend. But he refused a publicist, shunned his agent, and (apparently) didn't want a girlfriend. I was his boss—*just* his boss—and it was my job to write his character, not his press releases.

Plus, I already had a boyfriend. A very good boyfriend, Keith. Whose loyalty and friendship I also valued.

"Dallas is . . . great," I said. "Very professional."

Not the kind of dirt my makeup artist was hoping for. She let me know with a roundhouse powder puff to the face. I was done.

I coughed my way through the cloud and over to the watercooler to wash down the particles. Behind me someone sniped, "Way to be a cheerleader." I looked up and instantly wished I hadn't. It was Mom's disciple and my Judas, Alexis Randall, one of the two teen female leads on the show. "I hope you talk about me with the same enthusiasm you have for Dallas," she said, fluffing her hair.

"I love all my cast members equally, Alexis." *It's just the loathing I reserve for you.* "You look nice." *I'm thinking of writing you off my show.* "Ready for the big announcement?" *You will die in a hippopotamus mauling.* "I bet you get nominated."

And just like that, my name was love. "Do you really think so?" she squealed. "I spent weeks studying all my material to figure out what to submit to the judges. It's so hard when you have so much to choose from."

Barf. "You went with the scenes where Ryan and Sarah wait for the results of her pregnancy test, right? That stuff's gold."

"No," she said, surprised. "Everybody said the judges wouldn't pay much attention to me if I sent in scenes with Dallas. They said he's too distracting."

I looked at her cockeyed. "That episode was the most heartfelt we've ever seen Sarah. You went through a kajillion emotions in the course of five minutes, and Dallas did nothing but hold your hand."

Alexis shot me a glance. "You know as well as I do that he doesn't need lines to steal a scene."

Fair enough, I thought. "So what did you settle on?"

"My scenes with your mother. Where she counsels Sarah to convert to Wicca."

I laughed.

"What's wrong with that?"

"Nothing. It's just a bold choice, that's all. Academy voters tend to favor drama over comedy." Judging by the look on

Alexis's face, she found nothing funny about those scenes. "Plus," I scrambled, "if you're worried about getting overshadowed by anyone, it ought to be my mother. She makes a meal out of all her material. Even when her character's comatose."

Alexis squinted, revealing a flash of doubt. But it was just a flash. "I think your mother's presence in the scenes only elevates my game. We talked it over, and everyone agrees, even my fan club president. That stuff is my best shot."

I shrugged. What did I know? The only award I'd ever been nominated for was Most Likely to Punch a Girl.

Alexis's five-minute call was announced over the PA. She tossed her hair with renewed confidence and told me she wasn't worried. "Funny or not, *you* wrote it. And you're a shoo-in for a nomination, too."

I didn't think so, but kept it to myself. My team of whippersnappers was pitted against an industry full of writers who were seven times our age. Not one of them was going to vote for the kid whose upstart show had run off with the top spot in the ratings.

"I don't need any award to tell me I done good," I murmured, well after Alexis had left for the studio floor.

Hmm . . . then why did I feel the need to tell myself that? Out loud?

The nominations came fast and furious. Talk shows went first (*Blabbermouth* failed to nab a nom; its British ex-pat host was particularly put out when two minutes later he had to announce the cut for Best Home Plumbing Show).

I spent the commercial break gnawing on my fingernails

and was seconds from an emergency manicure when I felt a tap on my shoulder.

"Look at you, you're all nervous."

That voice. Like the sound of Christmas presents unwrapping. I caught my breath and turned.

"Nervous? *Moi?* This is just another day in the life, Dallas. Looking good, by the way."

Cynthia had lost the war (he was wearing clothes, after all) but had won a few battles. "Ya think?" Dallas asked. He did a 360 in his yellow tee and shredded stonewashed jeans. I nearly combusted at the 180 mark: One rip was right on the southern border of his butt. "It seems more like Javier's style, but the costumer says it's the new look. If I'd known, I would have worn boxers."

If he was aware of my reaction, he made no sign of it.

"Come on," he ribbed. "Look at that." Up on the stage flanking the podium were two human-size replicas of an Emmy. "You can't tell me you don't want one of those things for your bookshelf."

"My bookshelf is a place of dignity—of Dickinson, Blume, von Ziegesar. It sets a tone for my room that a gold-plated statuette would seriously tarnish."

Dallas crossed his arms in front of him, hitched up a satisfied smile, and sprung a trap. "So you *do* want one. It's just a matter of feng shui."

He's an actor, I kept trying to remind myself. *He's not supposed to have interests beyond self-promotion and self-absorption, much less an understanding of ancient Chinese design concepts. Why must he prove me wrong?* "My noninterest in awards season has less to do with furniture placement than it does with the Hayden family's sanity. You'd know that if you'd seen my mother this morning."

"I did, back at the studio . . . but I'm not sure she saw me. Or anyone else around her, for that matter. She looked like she'd been into Richard's Xanax."

"And the Vicodin and the Ativan," I said. "She has one thing on her mind, and one thing only: seeing her name among the nominated. Mom gets Emmy fever every year—and every year, when she doesn't get picked, it nearly kills her, not to mention innocent bystanders like me."

"But you aren't your mother."

"Thank you for saying so, but I could become her if I'm not careful. And so could you, if you buy into all this nonsense."

Somewhere the stage manager was calling places for the next segment, but Dallas made no move to leave. "It's always nice to be recognized," he suggested.

"Except by photographers when without makeup. Or going into rehab. Or coming out of a police station." I could have gone on, but Dallas put up his hands in mock surrender.

"Or onstage with your peers, who're applauding your incredible achievement," he said. "The horror, right?"

Dallas was called again.

"Maybe you should take your place," I said, growing uneasy with the attention.

"I get it," he said, backing away. "Some people don't like the limelight. And who wants an award when it'll only raise expectations? Being a sixteen-year-old head writer's hard enough, but an Emmy Award–winning sixteen-year-old head writer? Talk about pressure. You'd only be the most sought-after writer in LA. Worst thing ever." He stopped for a second, then added with a twinkle, "How about if I just want one for you?" He smiled a crooked smile and walked off.

Dallas wanted an award for me. That was kind of an award all by itself.

Stop knowing me so well, I thought.

It could only lead to a place neither of us could go.

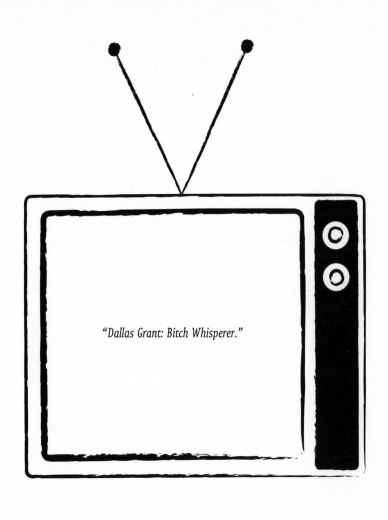

"Dallas Grant: Bitch Whisperer."

f o u r

As it turned out, Dallas was nominated for a Daytime Emmy of his own. The pool of candidates for Best Younger Actor was kiddie-pool shallow these days. Most guys his age swaggered into LA aiming for a lead in Gus Van Sant's latest, but ended up in a *Gossip Girl* spin-off as Frat Boy #2. Few bothered with soaps, which left the field wide open for Juilliard-trained Dallas. His closest competition was a towheaded eight-year-old who played a jive-talking leprechaun. If it bothered Dallas that his work would be judged against a second grader's, he had the class not to show it—he was all smiles when he bounded out a minute later to present the nominations for the next set of awards. Alexis, already out there, didn't share his enthusiasm, and it showed. Her dream had just been murdered. Brutally.

For Best Younger Actress, the nominees were: a hermaphrodite, a leper, a mermaid, and a *pregnant teenager* . . . but not Alexis's dramatic turn as a lapsed Catholic turned moon goddess. Her mic boosted the sound of her grinding teeth for all the studio audience to cringe at.

I tried hard not to enjoy it.

"Congratulations, Dallas," she eked out before perking up for the task at hand.

"Thank you very much, Alexis. And now for Best Actress in a Leading Role. The nominees are . . . Georgina Devereaux, *Travels of the Heart*" (surprise, surprise—she'd been nominated every year since 1952); "Anastasia Driscoll, *Wherefore Art Thou, Love?*" (another year, another broken heart, another nomination); "Westerly Easton, *The Dreaming and the Damned*" (for the moving tale of One Woman's Battle against shopping addiction); "and . . ."

The final name swung at me like a slap, and connected like a wrecking ball.

My mother. *Likely Story*.

"Congratulations to all the nominees," I heard Dallas say. At least I think that's what he said. I'm not sure. His words were muffled by the leather of my bag, into which I was dry-heaving.

My mother was at long last an Emmy nominee, after decades of snubbery.

Was it right to feel sick? Should I have been happy for her? Would the daughterly thing to do have been to stand up and cheer?

The pat on my back said, *What's good for Mom is good for all of us*. I wiped the drool from my mouth and looked up at *Likely Story*'s publicist, a feathery woman by the name of Kimberly Winters.

"Oh my God!" she exclaimed amidst the thrum of the applause and *Blabbermouth*'s closing credits. "This is fantastic! Are you excited?"

"Sure," I managed. "Mom deserves everything she's got coming to her." And then some.

"I'm not talking about your mom—I'm talking about you!"

I followed her sight line to the monitors hanging from the lighting grid above the stage. On them rolled the list of all this year's nominees. I'd been too busy keeping my lunch down to listen up for the announcement of "Best Writing: *All My Affairs, Between Heaven and Hell, Likely Story,* and *Tropical Hospital.*"

My jaw dropped, providing clearance enough for a jumbo jet. And then . . . "Best Show: *Good As Gold, Likely Story, Mason-Dixon,* and *The Walking Wounded.*"

My name.

My show.

Twice.

This had to be a conspiracy. It made no sense. We'd only been on the air for a couple of months. We barely made the cutoff for the nominating period! But we'd tallied four huge nominations. Was someone at the accounting agency stuffing the ballot boxes? Were the UN's election observers needed in Hollywood?

Then, a blur. *A Night on Bald Mountain* sounding on my cell phone, and Richard's name on the display. Kimberly tugging at my sleeve. Shoved into the press pen. Bombarded with questions. *How do you feel? Do you deserve it? What do you think about your mother? What will you wear? Do you deserve it?* Richard again. Alexis's evil eye, searing me from her *Entertainment Tonight* interview all the way across the floor. Collapsing into a chair in the greenroom, my head between my legs. Deep breaths. A sudden whiff of Tom Ford. Dallas.

"Congrats on the nomination," I groaned.

"Thank you. And my condolences to you."

"Since when are you smug?"

"Since I got to tell *Access Hollywood* that you have it in the bag." He handed me a bottle of Voss. "Sip."

I swigged. "You didn't."

"I most certainly did. And you do."

His conviction was positively priestly. But now I'd have to deliver a miracle.

"How can you be so sure?" I asked.

"You know what? You're totally right. When they asked me to handicap the race, I should have said, 'What are you, nuts? *Tropical Hospital*'s totally going to win for the monkey brain virus outbreak story.'"

I wanted to smile, but it *was* kind of an ace for *TH*. Half their cast spent all of May sweeps picking at each other's scalps in search of ticks.

"Some things you just get a feeling about."

"Let me know if you ever get a feeling about lotto numbers or tsunamis, Nostradamus."

"Prediction: You and your mom take home matching Emmys."

"You're so far off base you're in a hockey rink."

"Bet me," he dared.

"I don't think that would be appropriate for a head writer and one of her cast—"

"Chicken."

"Teach me to ride your hog," I blurted.

"Wha-at?"

"Your motorcycle, sicko. Don't bother denying it—I know

42

you have one, in flagrant violation of the personal risk clause in your contract. Francesca gave you up months ago in exchange for wardrobe approval."

Dallas's smile glinted off the lights. "She is so dead."

"If either Mom or I lose the Emmy, you have to teach me."

"And if you both win, Ryan has no pool scenes all summer. I've got gym fatigue—I need to give my body a rest without worrying about going shirtless for the camera."

I took that bet without a moment's thought. There were plenty of ways of getting Dallas shirtless without writing a pool scene. He figured that out one handshake too late. I told him not to worry.

"I can't imagine her winning. She's going to be absolutely insufferable with just a nomination." My cell rang. Richard again. "He's probably already planning the press conference." I sighed.

"For once, I can say I don't blame him."

I was not looking forward to the Mom/Richard double-team treatment tonight over dinner. No way were they going to let me take my curry to my room, not when they could discuss how to use me to secure my mother's win. I turned to Dallas.

"You free for dinner tonight?"

He grinned. "As long as I get to talk to the head writer about my dialogue for tomorrow. I'd like to make some changes."

No doubt about it, Dallas had shed any reservations he once had about joking around with me. I wondered if I was giving him those cues, or if he was taking them from me.

I answered the phone and rolled my eyes for Dallas. "Great news, right, Richard?"

"Yeah yeah yeah, I'm thrilled for you. You know who I just got a call from, Mallory?"

Again with the guessing games. "The Dalai Lama. He read *Soap Opera Digest* and he's pissed we're pairing Ryan with Jacqueline."

"Your principal."

Crap.

"You're late for gym."

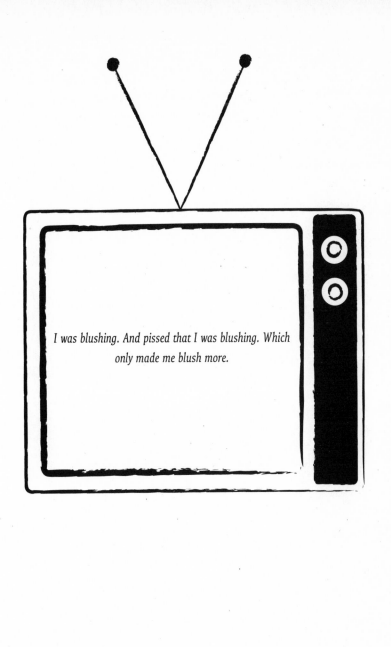

I was blushing. And pissed that I was blushing. Which only made me blush more.

f i v e

A shuttlecock is a lethal weapon.

This I learned when I burst into my school's gym crying "Here I am!" as if I'd be greeted like a conquering hero instead of a fink. Fortunately, growing up with Mom, I had plenty of experience dodging vases. I ducked the birdie and it dented the bleachers instead of my exceptionally thick skull.

"You're late, Hayden!" Coach Samson barked, swinging a regulation racquet.

"Yes, sir, Coach Samson, sir!"

"Let me ask you something, Hayden: Do you smell scented candles?"

Snickering from the peanut gallery. Guys and girls in Cloverdale uniforms stopped batting at each other and gawked, egged on by one familiar, odious voice in particular.

"She ought to, Coach," my ex–best friend, Amelia, cooed, in that pervily flirtatious voice that some girls use to get what they want from gym teachers. "She's got her nose up high enough in the air to smell ozone."

I kept my head held high, sure, but that was ridiculous. "Just sweat and floor wax, sir," I told Coach.

"Do you see massage tables or hot stones or waiters carrying wheatgrass juice?" he barked.

"Sir?"

"Does it look like I'm running a day spa?!"

"No, sir. It looks like you're running a Soviet prison camp."

This was just the excuse Coach needed to get right up in my face. "This is gym, my gym, and you do not get to stroll in whenever it suits you. Did or did not the principal send you a letter stating you were on the brink of flunking for missed classes? And did or did not that letter state that if your fancy-schmancy teevee show continued to interfere with your physical education, your work permit would be revoked?"

"Did, sir."

"Then I suggest you get a racquet and get to work!"

I pulled an envelope from my bag and used the too-close-for-comfort distance to conceal the handoff to Coach. "Maybe you should read my note, first." *Hint, hint.*

Coach glanced at the enclosed glamour shot of my mom circa 1991, forged by yours truly: *To Coach—love is all! XOXO.*

Suddenly cuddly, he whispered, "Sweet. Sorry for the yelling. I have to make it look good, right?"

"You were very convincing."

"Really? I've been taking classes at the Actors Studio."

"It shows. Keep it up and maybe there's a walk-on for you in the future. Just try not to take my head off with the shuttlecock next time, okay?"

"It got away from me, I swear. Don't be late next time,

okay? We're starting a new block, and everyone's expected to participate."

I gave him my word, because I knew the administration's smackdown was no joke. I'd managed to get decent grades since production of *Likely Story* began, and I'd thought no one would care if I ignored the daily jumping jacks requirement as long as I had some Dance Dance Revolution tournaments with Tamika in the privacy of the writers' room. But the Powers That Be were paying closer attention than I'd thought. It was one thing for me to juggle school and a show, quite another to juggle school, a show, and wacky hijinks, which I'd totally and very publicly done just a few months ago. And in this age of Girl Actresses Gone Bad, the school was not going to chance its reputation on me. That meant no free passes—and no way out of badminton.

It also meant Amelia.

"Hey, Mal," she trilled, spinning her racquet. *Ignore her,* I thought. "Wanna play?" *Be the bigger person.* "I feel like whacking at something ugly."

Oh, forget it. Just slam her. Resistance is futile.

"Well, Amelia, I wonder if your brother thinks the same thing every time he sees you in a bikini."

That ought to have shut her up, but my former best friend was scrappier than she used to be, and I had the scratches to prove it. She stuck out her racquet, barring my way.

"I can tell you one thing—he's sure not thinking about your skanky self." Obviously Amelia was unaware of Jake's clunky attempts to get his flirt on with me. File that under *Save for a Rainy Day.*

"That actually warms my heart," I responded. "Because every time Jake thinks about me, I feel like someone stepped on my grave."

"Like that would bother you. You won't stop until you have a guy wrapped around each of your grubby little fingers."

A gentle hand snaked around my waist, pulled me close, and said with authority, "She's happy with just one, I promise." One lips-to-neck graze, and then, "Hey, Daisy."

"Hey, Gatsby," I beamed.

Keith had superheroic timing. It wasn't like I needed rescuing, but it was nice to know he was always around should I find myself tied to some train tracks. Or just too exhausted to fight every single one of my own battles. I wondered if that made me a sorry excuse for a girl of the newish millennium.

Amelia dug in her heels. "I can't believe you still buy her act, Keith."

Keith shrugged. "What can I say? She puts on a good show."

"Kind of makes you wonder if anyone else is getting tickets, doesn't it?"

My inner prompter signaled: *Exit stage right, right the hell now.*

"Do us all a favor and leave the extended metaphors to us professionals, okay?" I said, tugging at Keith.

But Amelia was just warming up. Like all best-of-friends-turned-enemies, she knew my sore spots, and because I used to tell her all my dirty little secrets, she knew Keith's, too. "Seriously, Keith. How long before you think Mallory takes a page from your book and starts seeing someone like, oh I don't know, *Dallas* on the side? Maybe she already is. Why don't you ask your crazy ex-girlfriend, Erika, for pointers? I bet she knows all the signs of a cheater by heart."

Keith pulled free of me and turned on Amelia. "Do you have to be so hateful?"

The big doof thought he could shame her. But Amelia and I had thrown both food and punches. Neither one of us had much dignity left.

I couldn't blame her for holding a grudge. Just last year I'd done the unthinkable: promised her the lead role in *Likely Story,* only to turn around and give it to Alexis (who was a bitch, but at least was a bitch with talent). When Amelia lost the part, she also felt she'd lost her standing. One minute she was leaving high school behind; the next, I was leaving her in my dust. When it had come down to my show or my friend, I'd chosen my show and had hoped Amelia would understand.

No such luck. Amelia saw no silver lining, just Hurricane Mallory tearing the roof off her life. There would be no more IM'ing, no more Jack in the Box runs, no more ripping on my mother. Just the resentment that stays when everything else goes.

I could see the next line of attack forming on her face, but she was interrupted by my soapfan sidekick Scooter, who ran in and tackled me, landing us both on the floor.

"I AM SO PSYCHED!" he shouted. "ARE YOU?!"

"I'm sure I will be, once I can breathe again," I gasped.

Scooter rolled off and helped Keith pull me up. "I guess I don't know my own strength," he said, vibrating with excitement. "I can't believe you even came to class today. Shouldn't you be giving interviews and strategizing and stuff?"

Keith looked puzzled. "What am I missing?" he asked. Meanwhile, Amelia pursed her lips like she was offended at having her reaming upstaged, instead of dying to know what Scooter was bouncing about.

Coach stormed up. "Why do I see dillydallying instead of driving and smashing?"

Scooter took my hand and thrust it forward. "Because," he uttered triumphantly, "this is the hand of Daytime Royalty, and it is far too delicate to risk getting all callused playing Ping-Pong."

"Badminton," Coach corrected.

"Whatever," said Scooter. "The point is, Mallory can't accept Emmys with gnarled cuticles, right?"

Keith and Amelia swung looks at me. Coach dropped all pretense.

"No way! You're nominated?!"

"Yeah," I squeaked. "Weird, huh?"

"It doesn't stop there," chimed my one-man PR machine. "So's her mom!"

Coach was staggered. "It's about time! I thought she was a shoo-in the year Geneva gave herself an emergency appendectomy with a butter knife."

"Or when her plane crashed in the veldt and she faced down a pride of lions with nothing but a plunger and her sense of self-worth!" topped Scooter.

"Or when she drove the hydrofoil through Bruce and Penelope's wedding to stop Cruiser from stopping it himself!"

I knew this could go on forever.

I wanted it to stop.

I turned away from Coach and Scooter's bonding moment

and sized up Keith, wondering what sort of apology was in order for not calling him right away with the news. Or for neglecting, in the first place, to tell him the nominations were happening today. Or for just being a sucky girlfriend, which covered the first two and whatever else I might do wrong before the day was done.

"What about Alexis?" Amelia demanded to know.

"What about her?"

"Did she get nominated or what?"

"I'm afraid she didn't. That totally alien, warm, and tingly feeling creeping up your bones is called vindication. So get it out of your system. Tell me how everything would've been different if only you'd been playing Sarah instead of her."

Amelia hadn't held her tongue once so far and wasn't going to start now. "If you really need me to tell you that, then we were never friends in the first place." She turned on her heel and sped off like she'd been called to arms. I hated surrendering the last word to Amelia, but Keith was waiting for an explanation. He'd have to wait a little longer, because Coach blew his whistle and hollered at the class to bring it in.

"Listen up! Today marks the end of our badminton unit. Come next class we'll be starting something new."

"Coed mud wrestling?" hooted one football player. A blind person could have seen the collective eyes rolling.

"Nope, don't even bother changing into your uniforms. We're going to be square-dancing," responded Coach.

No one said a word. I raised my hand.

"I think I speak for all of us when I ask, what's so wrong with coed mud wrestling?"

Coach told the angry mob to settle down. "It wasn't my

decision. The ladies on the school board are wrinkling as we speak, worried about all the bumping and grinding observed at the Valentine's Day dance. They're out to teach you kids there are other ways to show affection, not to mention some manners. I could have told them you're a lost cause, but nobody listens to me. Now hit the showers."

I turned toward Keith, but he was already retreating toward the guys' locker room.

"Meet you outside" was all he said.

I made a descent into the heart of darkness—the girls' locker room. I sequestered myself in a dank little corner and changed out of my hideous gym clothes. I was tying my shoes when Amelia's voice wafted over the din of gossip. I didn't want to listen. I tried not to. But the more she spoke, the less everyone else did. If she'd fallen from grace since we'd de-friended, she'd since climbed back up even higher than she'd been before.

"Mallory was always that way," she pontificated. "Self-righteous and full of herself. I just never saw it, because she never directed any of it at me. She was that girl who would sit around and make fun of what people wore to school. And her attitude's only going to get worse now that she's up for that stupid award. If only those people who voted for her knew what she was really like."

I double-, triple-, and quadruple-knotted my shoelaces, just to give myself time enough to listen to Amelia talk smack. Any more and I'd cut off circulation to my feet. I got up to go.

"And the thing is," she went on, safe behind a bank of lockers but totally aware I was hearing all of it, "she doesn't even know why they chose her. She thinks it's because she's a good writer. As if. It wasn't even her idea to put her mom on the show, and that was, like, the best move she could have made. The only reason she's nominated is because they couldn't afford to ignore her. She's the most famous thing soaps have going for them. But no way will she win. What would look better on camera? A sixteen-year-old nerd getting an award and jumping up and down onstage . . . or the look on her face when she loses to a story about a killer mime?"

The sheep laughed in unison. So did I, actually, as I walked out. It was funny. And then I started to feel a lump in my throat. Because it was also true.

Keith was waiting for me at his Mustang, wiping down the fender of the car he'd spent ages painstakingly restoring. I used to wonder how anyone could spend that much time on one project without going crazy. You'd think that with *Likely Story* in my life, I'd have stopped wondering. But I was as curious as ever.

I'd donned shades hoping to avoid the "Is something wrong?" conversation. It worked, mostly.

"You're all puffy, Minneapolis."

"Let's just go, St. Paul."

If it had been *Likely Story*, and I was Jacqueline, and Keith was Ryan, he wouldn't have let me get in the car. He would've asked me what was wrong and wouldn't have taken "allergies" or some other lamery for an answer. I'd have poured out my heart in fits and starts, and he'd say the perfect thing and I'd feel revived. At least until the next episode.

But Keith wasn't Ryan. He was my high school boyfriend, and despite all of the awesome qualities that made him the greatest catch at Cloverdale, he was still just a boy. And like all boys, he had no idea how to handle a girl who'd been crying. I might as well have sat him down in front of a sewing machine and told him to make me a Dior.

He parked the car in front of my house, and as the engine wound down, we had a relationship first: a moment when neither one of us knew what to say.

"So what exactly is an Emmy?" Keith asked.

"A winged muse carrying an atom." I hated that I knew that.

"Art and science coming together. Sounds pretty cool." He sighed heavily.

"Are you pissed at me?" I asked, unable to stand it.

"Of course not—I thought you were pissed at *me*! I was waiting all day to hear the news, and then when you didn't call me, I figured I'd backed up over your dog or something."

"But you don't even know what an Emmy is," I said, mystified.

"But I'd have to be an extremely incompetent boyfriend not to know they were happening today . . . even if you didn't want me to know." He reached into the backseat and produced a bouquet of flowers. "Congratulations," he said with a smile.

Roses, the mark of an expert. Now for the sorry, the mark of an amateur.

"Thank you. And I'm a jerk," I moaned. "I just didn't think you'd appreciate me calling with more news about *Likely Story* while you were stuck in class."

Keith admitted with no hesitation that the show was not his favorite subject. "But you *are*," he said. "So I don't mind hearing about it, even if it means having to talk about your mom or Amelia or Richard. Or even Dallas." I was going to kill

Amelia. We'd gone a good two months without a Dallas mention, but her sniping had obviously gotten to Keith. She could aggravate a Zen master right into a screaming fit.

Keith started the car. "Let's celebrate. Picnic at Malibu."

"That sounds fantastic . . . but I can't. I've got this dinner thing with Mom and Richard." His eyes started to glaze over. Obviously he didn't mind hearing about *Likely Story*, just so long as he didn't have to listen. "Work and Emmys and all that." And Dallas. But now was definitely not the time to put that name back into play. "How about if I see you one picnic and raise you a black-tie awards ceremony?"

Keith agreed, but only if he didn't have to wear a bow tie. And only if he got a Hollywood kiss, to boot. The guy had no future in show business. The only things he ever asked of me were things I'd freely give.

Putting my foot down would be meaningless if I couldn't hold my ground.

s i x

An hour later I sat down in front of my computer, freshly showered, changed, and scented. Hours-old IMs peppered my screen from friends long since signed off. GinaBeana wrote: *Good for you! You're going to win it! Can I do your makeup?* BruinBoy, my one true ally at the network, Greg, had this: *You're so rocking these awards.* My e-mail overflowed with congratulatory notes from my agent and all manner of network execs (delete, delete, delete), not to mention a few conspicuous messages from cast members who hadn't had a lot of airplay lately. ("Hey, good for you with the Emmys. I've got tons of ideas for [insert my character name here]. Let's talk about it over lunch!")

Nestled among the usual stuff was this:

TO: MALLORY HAYDEN (malcontent@likelystory.com)
FROM: FAN CLUB PRESIDENT (fanclub@alexisrandall.com)
SUBJECT: A New Direction

This, I had to read.

Ms. Hayden,

Why do you hate Alexis? You must have a grudge against her to write so much bad story so she doesn't get a nomination. Her work has been amaing, even when she did not have the best writing to work with. We in the fan club have a few suggestions we'd like to share for future story. How about putting her back with Ryan? Alexis and Dallas have great chemistry. A psycho cray person could kill off Jacqueline, and Sarah could help him get over her. Maybe you are not the right person to write for Alexis's talent. Maybe

Delete. If this was Tamika's idea of a practical joke, she deserved a raise. If it wasn't, I needed to change my e-mail address.

My cell rang. It was my mother . . . calling from downstairs.

"Dallas is here," she said with her patented brew of perturbed confusion. "Did you invite him over for dinner?"

"Tell him I'll be right down."

"You know I don't like surprises, Mallory."

"That's strange. You sure love surprising *me*. Like when, surprise surprise, you secretly got a job on my show. And when, surprise surprise SURPRISE, you got engaged to my boss. And when—"

"I'll set another place."

"Try to be polite, Mom. And if that's too big a stretch, just leave us alone."

"I always mind my manners, Mallory. I sent him upstairs a moment ago."

"Mallory?" I heard from down the hall. I hung up on my mom and poked my head out the door as a bewildered Dallas walked out of the recital room (used briefly during my mother's ill-fated foray into classical guitar). "How many rooms are there in this place?"

"One for each of my mother's foul moods. As you can imagine, we're still adding on. The next room's either a meat smoker or a Pilates studio—I can't remember which."

Dallas stood at the threshold of my bedroom. "So this is your lair. Gonna give me the tour?"

I let him in, against my better judgment. It wasn't that the place was a war zone; I kept it immaculate (a tidy bedroom is the sign of a procrastinating writer). I worried a glimpse at my room might tell him too much about me. *See, this is my desk, where I IM you from. And here's my nightstand, where I keep notepads in case I wake up in the middle of the night with inspiration for a story for you. Oh, and this is my bed, where I have that recurring dream about you.*

Any of those things would've been easier to talk about than the contents of my bookshelf, which is what he zeroed in on. "I see plenty of room here for awards. Just relocate the Hello Kitty alarm clock and you're golden."

"Nobody messes with Hello Kitty."

"My bad," he said, backing off with a sly smile . . . onto my bed. "So, would now be a good time to go over my script questions with you?"

I groaned. "I thought you were joking before."

"I was. But then I was in makeup with Francesca and Alexis, and we got to talking about some scenes coming up later this week. It ends up that Francesca and I have completely different takes on them."

Dallas almost never talked to me about dialogue, and

definitely never asked questions. Francesca told me it was some code they lived by in the theater, "Honor the written word." In TV, it was "Honor the whims of those who hold the purse strings." I'd make it a point to hire more theater actors in the future. Dallas handed me a few pages. It was a beach scene with Ryan and Jacqueline.

> JACQUELINE
> I just want you to know how I feel.

> RYAN
> I think I know. You don't have to say it.

> JACQUELINE
> Don't you want to be on the same page?

> RYAN
> I don't think talking's necessarily going to get us there. Different words mean different things to different people. I know what you want to say. That you love me. I want to say the same thing. I just don't know if I know what it really means yet.

                    JACQUELINE
            So what do we do in the
                    meantime?

                       RYAN
        There's this. (HE KISSES HER)

                    JACQUELINE
        (SMILING) Sometimes actions
        aren't a good substitute for
                     words.

                       RYAN
        Maybe we need a code . . .
        until we both know we have
        the same definition for what
               we're feeling.

                    JACQUELINE
             (AN IDEA) Ryan . . . I
                loathe you.

                       RYAN
        I loathe you, too, Jacqueline.
             (ON THEIR KISS, FADE)

   "I'm a little confused," said Dallas. "We've been building
up to this huge moment between the two of them, but then
when they finally get there, they pull back. What gives? I
didn't think Ryan was the type to hide his feelings."

"You're right, he totally isn't."

"Well, don't they love each other?"

"Of course."

Dallas laughed in aggravation. "Then what's the big deal? Shouldn't he be shouting it from the rooftops?"

"If he was on *Tropical Hospital,* he would be. But the kids on that show also run international crime syndicates. This is *Likely Story.* Our kids are kids."

"What does that have to do with anything? A lot of kids don't think twice about throwing around the L-word."

"And doesn't that drive you crazy? Don't you ever wonder how anybody in high school can know what that word means? That none of them stop to think that using it so gratuitously at the age of sixteen might water it down for their whole lives to come? Did you ever say you loved someone when you were in high school?"

This question rendered him speechless. I rushed to fill the void. "Sorry! Way too personal. What Ryan's really trying to say in this scene is that he wants that word to count for something when he says it to Jacqueline for the first time. And I promise you, he will. He's not being standoffish or cold or brutal. It's the opposite. He's being careful with her feelings . . . and with his."

He smiled. "I think I get it. Thanks."

I wondered how much he really got it. But that would have to stay in the realm of the unsaid.

"Hey," I told him, "if we stay up here any longer, Richard's going to get all the vindaloo. Ready to do battle?"

Dallas nodded and told me to lead the way.

———

Dinner started off civilly enough. We ate outside in the gazebo, a thing we hadn't done since Mom's last divorce party. She'd lit up her marriage certificate in a vodka-fueled ecstasy; the resulting blaze nearly burned down the house and was dubbed "the opening of this year's wildfire season" by the local news.

For a while it was a *Likely Story* love-in. Mom and Richard patted themselves on the back for their success in the nominations. Dallas played along, and they showed him their love. Richard was keen to capitalize on the show's good fortune. "We can't afford to let this success make us complacent. That's the danger of these awards. They make you fat. Slow. Stupid. We have to use it. The network will be looking for us to follow it up with something big, something to keep our names in the news," he said, like he was the wise old sensei and I was the puckish young ninja.

"A scandal," my mother proposed.

"A story," Richard countered.

I helped myself to some more poori and pricked up my ears. Richard was ruminating about the show's next steps, which meant I had to be one step ahead of him or else we'd end up with an alien-baby story or, even worse, stunt casting.

I thought that by keeping quiet, I was keeping my head down. But apparently my silence was deafening. And somewhere between the tandoori and the tikka, Mom spoke up.

"Mallory doesn't care for all the Emmy talk," she confided, as though describing a museum exhibit.

"I don't mind it at all," I said. "I just prefer to let the three of you hash it out on your own."

"Why is it that you don't want to participate?" asked Richard, pushing it. "Afraid you'll jinx yourself?"

"Aren't *you*? There's a lifetime of Emmy history—or non-history, more like it—sitting right here at this table. You might want to think about taking that into consideration before you concoct your drive for votes."

Mom tutted. "One has to advertise oneself. That's the way it's done."

"And your mantel full of awards to prove that is where, exactly?" The sudden chill in the air was cold enough to freeze mercury. But there was no going back now. And I wouldn't even if I could. Somebody needed to get through to my mother, and it certainly wasn't going to be her fanboy boy toy.

"Why don't you just come out and call the pot a spade?" Mom asked, folding her napkin and setting it aside. "I haven't won, much less been nominated, because I'm an awful actress—"

"I don't think that's what she said at all," Dallas interrupted.

I shot him a look, warning him not to get involved. If blood was to be spilled, I didn't want it to be his.

"What I am trying to say," I said through gritted teeth, "is that there is no way to guarantee anything. Not with publicity and certainly not with talent. That's why I don't pay any attention to these things."

"Oh please," said Richard. "That's a pathetic cop-out. If you don't want to admit you want to win, fine, I get it. But don't pretend to be above it all."

"Who's pretending?" I said.

"Are you trying to tell us," Richard said, shaking his head, "that you won't be crushed if *All My Affairs* beats you with their 'Melinda Goes to Space Camp' story? Or that thing with the homicidal clown on *Between Heaven and Hell*?"

I was blushing. And pissed that I was blushing. Which only made me blush more. "It's a mime, not a clown. And it's hardly ever about who really deserves to win," I insisted. "It's about which show has the most employees to vote for their people, or who it'll look good for, or who'll bring in the ratings."

"Let me get this straight," my mother said. "You *do* deserve to win, but you won't, because there's a conspiracy against you?"

"What's *your* excuse?" Dallas challenged, taking his life in his hands. "You were the star of *Good As Gold* since before I was born. And in all those years of submitting yourself for approval, how many times did you get nominated?"

Mom cleared her throat. "Never."

"So what's different this time? Is it your acting? Have you been phoning it in for the last twenty-five years?"

"I've never given anything but my all to every scene," she vowed. "When Geneva psychically communed with porpoises off the coast of Bora-Bora? I made it my business to know everything there was to know about those fish, from blowhole to flippers. When those lunatic writers had her have an affair with the Sultan of Luxor, only to discover he was a three-thousand-year-old mummy with a Viagra dependency, you can bet your life I knew my Tutankhamen from my Akhenaton. You *children* have it easy—you just have to play yourselves. I, on the other hand, had to be *globally accurate*."

"Then maybe Mallory's right," Dallas said. "Maybe it doesn't matter how many parties you throw or gifts you send out. Maybe people don't vote for you because they just don't like you."

Mom didn't bat an eye. "You naive little boy, with your ridiculous four years of theater training and your paltry life experience! I don't know how it's done in New York, but here in Hollywood, *no one likes anyone*. One has contracts, not friends. Agents, not confidants. The minute you begin to think otherwise is the minute you get stabbed in the back."

The sad thing was, she really believed this to be true. "Then why do you want it, Mom?" I had to ask. "If you really think these people don't care about you or your work, why does it matter?"

She looked stunned. Like I'd asked her if Nielsen ratings came from the stork.

"Because an award is still an award, no matter who gives it or why. Roses don't grow on trees, you know. You have to get validation wherever you can."

I stood up from the table, tired of all this. "I'd settle for some validation from my own family once in a while." I took two steps and turned around to snark in my best approximation of her bitchy tone, "Congratulations, Mallory."

Then, before I could stalk off, she channeled my own voice and threw a "Congratulations, *Mom*" right back at me.

She had me down cold.

Dallas caught up with me in the front yard, and I found myself apologizing for the umpteenth time today, this time for running out on him.

"I'd call it more of a dramatic exit," he said. "And I should know—you write them for me all the time."

"I don't know why I let her get to me."

"I don't think you need a reason. She's your mom. She's designed to do that."

"Does yours do the same thing?" I asked, doubtful.

"Are you kidding? Up until I landed *Likely Story,* my mom was sure I'd wind up a waiter, if not a bum. She wanted me to be a doctor."

I could see it—Dallas in a white lab coat and scrubs, making rounds, listening to his patients confess their fears, or holding their hands or saving their lives. I could see him as anything, I realized. Maybe that's what made him such a good actor.

"The thing about my mom is," he said, "she's never been able to admit she's wrong. When I got the job with the show, she sent me a card telling me how proud she was . . . but she was sure to say, 'PS, if it doesn't work out, there's always med school.' Once I saw that, I realized that nothing I do will change her mind. And if I kept trying, we'd just fight our way through the rest of our lives."

"Does she keep harping on you to do something more productive with your life?" I inquired.

"Not as much. It's hard to argue with success. But I can tell she'd prefer I was healing the sick."

"So basically she's being passive-aggressive and you're rolling over."

We stopped at the end of the driveway.

"I'm picking my battles," he said. "And I happen to know that the only way to win that one is to lose my mom."

I wouldn't have minded losing my mom at that moment.

But now I had to add Dallas to the growing chorus of voices telling me to make nice with her. It was one thing to scoff at Richard and tune out Tamika, but ignoring Dallas was next to impossible.

My inner conflict must have been pretty outer, because Dallas winced like he'd slammed a car door on my pinkie. "I should've kept my mouth shut back there. Somehow I know to keep my counsel around my own mom, but not around other people's."

I let him off the hook. "If you hadn't piped up, I'd have antagonized her all on my own. That's how we roll in the Hayden house."

He looked at me intently. "I think it's amazing that you've survived sixteen years without her worst qualities rubbing off on you."

I thought of Amelia, who might die laughing at this. And Keith, who might not laugh, but might not argue, either.

"Trust me, you haven't seen either one of us at our worst. Stick around and watch what happens when we fight over the remote. The fur will fly."

"Let me know if you ever need a tag-team partner. It's fun going toe-to-spiked-heel with your mom."

"Until she walks all over you."

"We didn't do too bad holding our own. We'd have KO'd her instantly if we'd hit her with our secret weapon."

"What secret weapon?"

He leaned in close—kissing-distance close—and whispered in my ear. "The secret weapon is that she and I both know the only reason we got nominated is because of you. Without your stories, we'd be nothing. And I didn't use it, because you're the one who has to live with her, not me. So I'm leaving it up to you to pull the trigger. If that's what you want to do."

But was there any way for me to tell him what I *really* wanted to do?

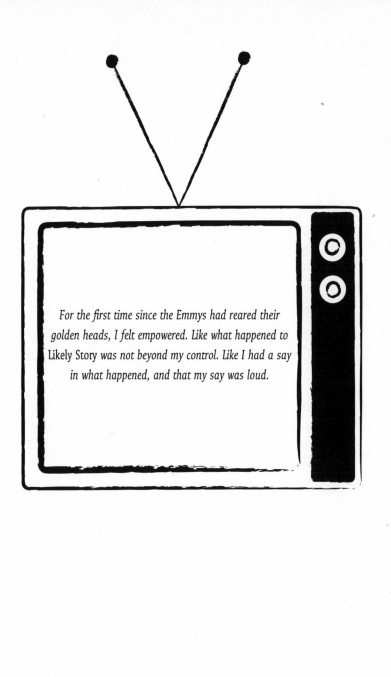

For the first time since the Emmys had reared their golden heads, I felt empowered. Like what happened to Likely Story was not beyond my control. Like I had a say in what happened, and that my say was loud.

s e v e n

Jammed under my door the next morning was a printed-out e-mail, no note attached.

FOR IMMEDIATE RELEASE:
NETWORK HONORED WITH TWENTY-TWO DAYTIME EMMY NOMINATIONS!
DAYTIME ROOKIE SENSATION "LIKELY STORY" HITS THE GROUND RUNNING WITH MULTIPLE NOMINATIONS!
The network congratulates Executive Producer Richard Showalter and Head Writer Mallory Hayden, creator of Likely Story, for a phenomenal showing. Among the awards their show is up for: Best Younger Lead Actor, Best Actress in a Leading Role, Best Writing, and Best Daytime Drama!

The next part was underlined in red pen.

When asked to comment on Likely Story's accomplishment, Marilyn Kinsey of Soap Opera Summary said this: "Story. Plain and simple. Mallory Hayden is a fresh, courageous voice in the world of soaps. Her ideas are original and her characters are bold—and Real. She's bringing people back to daytime, and for once the Academy is rewarding fine work and not the same old drivel that we've all become accustomed to."

I wiped the sleep from my eyes, briefly considering the identity of my anonymous fax-deliverer. The red pen was Mom's weapon of choice, but she had no motive for making nice. Richard needed my cooperation, though. And to get that, he needed me to believe we were all on the same side.

Maybe I'd been mellowed by the rare five straight hours of sleep I'd gotten. Maybe it was Dallas's advice and the plan it had spawned taking hold. Whatever it was, instead of shredding Richard's mea culpa, I folded it in two and put it in my bag. This, I figured, was the closest thing to praise I'd ever get from him.

"Pears?" Tamika sniffed when I got to the writers' room. "This is how the network says 'good for you'? Pears?"

The cast sent champagne.

The crew sent flowers.

Heck, the fans sent cookies (along with hundreds of postcards imploring us to keep Ryan and Jacqueline together).

But the network sent fruit.

"No bananas," I noted. "At least they're consistent."

Tamika read the card aloud for the rest of the writers to hear. " 'To our favorite scribes: Please enjoy "the fruits" of your labors!' "

The din of groans belied the fact that my staff was bouncing with excitement. They all wanted to win. I tried to tell them not to get their hopes up, that an Emmy was just a gold paperweight—and not even solid gold, just gold plate—but I got a barrage of spitballs for my efforts.

"We need optimism," cried Anna, my go-to girl for fantasy scenes.

"We need Fearless Leadership, not a Fearful Follower," said scriptwriter Ronald.

Who was I to ruin their fun?

The boss, that's who.

"All right, people, settle down," I begged in my best bio teacher persona (only to get more spitballs). "We've got a job to do—and thanks to these stupid Emmys, the pressure's on."

I told them about how Richard was looking to shake up the status quo and how my mother was egging him on. Though it was obvious to all of us that the show didn't need any revamping, I knew they had a point that our Network Overlords would agree with: We had to take advantage of the publicity while we had it.

"So I came up with something last night that will hopefully keep the show in news cycles, keep my mother out of our collective hair, *and* solve the murder mystery that we were saddled with on day one." I paused, aware that to speak it would be to give it life. This would be my Dr. Frankenstein moment. I just had to hope my own monster wouldn't kill me. "We're going to make my mother a murderer. And then we're going to murder *her*."

Half an hour later, Tamika walked me down the hall toward Richard's office for a quick pitch before the story meeting. In other circumstances, a trip to Richard's den might have been a death march. But this time I was treating it like a victory parade.

"You're strutting," Tamika observed.

"I don't strut."

"If you didn't before, you are now. Have you got 'Lady Marmalade' on repeat in your head?"

"What's wrong with confidence? I have to project power to wield power."

She yanked me into the copy room. "You're projecting more than power. You are aglow. Did you and Keith . . . ?"

"What, are you crazy? That's, like, a whole high school graduation away from now, if even then. I had no time to even think about Keith last night, much less *that*. Between Mom and Richard and Dallas and writing and—"

"Excuse me, *Dallas*?"

Damn it all. Had it been anyone else but Tamika, I might have been able to play this off.

"And how does young Mr. Grant fit into your evening?" she pursued.

"I invited him over to dinner last night," I said. Tamika sighed. "For moral support," I quickly added.

"If you wanted someone to back you up with Richard and your mom, you could have called me. Or Keith. Why Dallas?"

"Because Richard would have made sport out of taking you apart, and I won't have my mother forgetting Keith's name to his face for the fourth time," I sputtered. "But neither Richard nor my mother can afford to alienate Dallas, so I asked him. How about giving me a little credit, huh? There's nothing going on between Dallas and me. I have a boyfriend. Okay?"

"Whoa. When did I say something was up with you and Dallas?"

"You were thinking it," I insisted.

"The only thing I was thinking was 'God help her if the rest of the cast finds out Dallas has the head writer's ear.' Now I'm thinking, 'God help her if they find out he's got her heart, too.'"

"You need a vacation," I said dismissively. "You've got soap opera on the brain."

"Maybe it's monkey brain virus," she said, letting it go. "If you say it isn't so, I trust you. But not everybody's going to take your word for it. Especially when you protest too much."

My phone rang. "It's Keith," I said.

"You're going to take it, right?"

"Of course! Why wouldn't I?"

"Just checking," Tamika said. "Talk on the way. Richard's waiting."

"Hey, Batman," I said into my phone. "How goes it?"

"Hey. I just wanted to check in and see how you're doing. You sound pretty perky. I guess everything went okay with dinner last night."

"Ugh. Not really. Dinner itself was a bust. That's what I get for breaking bread with my enemies."

"Sounds like you could have used some reinforcements."

"Yeah, but you'd have hated it."

"How do you know?" he asked. "Maybe I like spending time with my girlfriend, even if it means having to spend time with her mother."

"And her boss, and her job, and all the stupid awards talk?" I asked, stopping outside Richard's office. "Come on, you'd have been climbing the walls. Plus, we had Indian. Your pizza-trained stomach couldn't have taken it."

There was a little noise from his end, like a cough or a snort.

"Anyway, I survived and even managed to get some inspiration out of it. So it wasn't all bad."

"That's all you got? Inspiration?"

"What else would I get?"

"I don't know," he said with an air of impatience. "You're the writer. You tell me."

I was a writer, not a mind reader. "Is everything okay?"

"I'm not having such a hot day," he admitted.

Richard poked his head out from his office. "Is there a reason you're having a conversation right outside my door? Are you trying to advertise your boyfriend issues?"

I told Keith to hang on a sec. "I need to talk to you," I said to Richard. "Story. Publicity. Big ratings."

"Next time, lead with 'big ratings,' " he said. "Come in, sit down, and talk fast. The network's on its way."

"Hey, Keith?" I asked.

"Don't tell me. You have to go."

"See you at square dancing, partner?"

"Yeah, sure," he mumbled.

"Hold up a second. You do know who Batman is, right? Dark Knight, cape, gadgets . . . youthful sidekick named Robin?"

"Yeah. Look, you'd better go. Richard needs you. Catch you later." He hung up. Every conversation we'd had since we were a "we" had included our nickname game. This was the first time in our history that he'd failed to play. I tried not to think about what that meant, but I didn't have to try hard. The network had arrived. Trip Carver (President of Daytime), Frieda Weiner (Network Consultant for Daytime Brand Management), and Greg were filing into Richard's office for the story meeting.

Keith would have to wait.

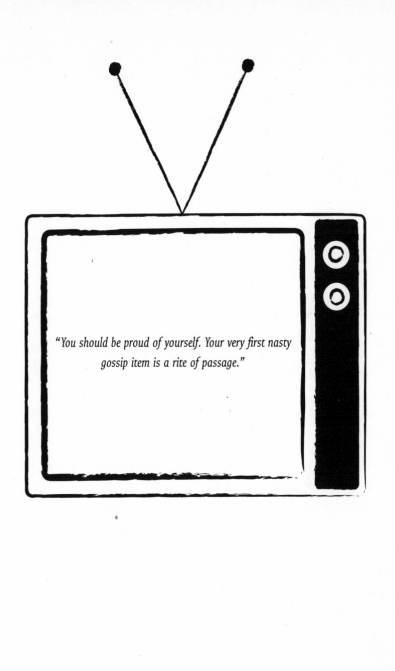

"You should be proud of yourself. Your very first nasty gossip item is a rite of passage."

e i g h t

"So?" asked Trip, whipping out his BlackBerry and crossing his legs. "What have you got for us?" That was it. No comment on the nominations. No pleasantries. Barely even a hello. I remembered Mom's take on the subject at dinner last night and hoped I'd never have occasion to tell her she was right. It was like the execs were afraid a kind word would put them at my mercy. And what did they think I would do if it did? Make them sit, stay, and speak for a treat?

And then there was Greg. He'd yet to be co-opted by the suits he slaved away for. He still knew how to be a human being. "Did you get the fruit basket?" he asked. "I argued for the Espresso and Valium package from Coffee Bean, but lost."

"Nonetheless, we're very grateful," I said, winking to him before facing the rest of the table. "Thanks very much from all the writers for your thoughtful gift."

Frieda reminded Trip that they had a sales presentation with the product placement people in thirty. "In Santa Monica," she warned.

"Then we'll be brief," said Richard. "Let's hear it, Mallory."

Trip was punching away at his BlackBerry, challenging me to get his attention. Under other circumstances I'd have taken this disrespect in stride, but my idea was designed to appeal directly to his sensibilities, not to mention his status as one of my mother's coterie of ex-husbands. I couldn't pitch to Frieda—she pooh-poohed anything that she hadn't already consulted on—and Greg had no power. I could look to him for support, but not for a go-ahead.

"I'm killing my mother."

That got their attention.

"Can I get in on that?" asked Trip with a smile—the opposite of Richard's expression. Richard was practically baring his teeth in a snarl.

"I thought you might like that, Trip. It's going to be brutal, too."

"Tell me more," said Trip, his PDA now in his pocket.

"Yes, Mallory," Richard chimed in. "Let's hear how you plan to pull this off."

Just for good measure, I threw in, "Are you sure you have time, Trip? We could pick this up after your meeting."

Trip told Greg to cancel with Sales. "I want to give my favorite former stepdaughter all my concentration."

I spent twenty minutes taking them through the plot, point by point. We would reveal that Mom's character, Vienna, was not being hidden by the government, she was hiding *from* the government. She was wanted in ten states on charges of fraud and extortion.

"We'll have Sarah figure it out when she confronts Vienna

about all the terrible advice she's given as her guidance coun-selor," I said.

"Like, to convert to Wicca," confirmed Frieda.

"Or that you can't get pregnant the first time. Or that it's okay to wear white after Labor Day. Whatever. We've been playing Vienna as a dope from day one. There's plenty of mate-rial for that. So Sarah goes to Vienna."

> SARAH
> How many other lives have you
> ruined with your stupid
> advice?

> VIENNA
> (INNOCENT) You're a happier
> person thanks to me.

> SARAH
> My mother's going to disown
> me! Ryan broke up with me!
> How can you call yourself a
> guidance counselor?

> VIENNA
> I don't, actually. (ON
> SARAH'S HORROR, FADE)

"Vienna's big secret is that she isn't accredited?" asked Richard, rolling his eyes.

"Hardly," I replied. "Vienna reveals her MO. She becomes the guidance counselor at the local high school of wherever she's at. She befriends the students who come to her with their secrets . . . and then she blackmails them."

"Secrets they'd *kill* to keep," Greg added, onto me.

"Exactly," I said. "And that's when Sarah goes berserk and murders Vienna."

This sent the room into a tizzy.

"Are we firing Alexis, too?!" cried Frieda, appalled.

"We've already got one unsolved murder on the show, now you want a second?" asked Richard, apoplectic.

"It's not that big a deal," I assured them, "because Sarah committed both murders."

Even Greg exclaimed "No way!" at that one.

"Sarah killed the student council president in episode one?" he asked.

"I think the pressing question is—Sarah's a double freaking murderer?" spit Richard.

I was ready for reservations. I'd come prepared for combat. "Look, no one knows who killed that kid. I don't even know, and I'm the head writer! It was not my idea to start the show off with a murder, but what's done is done, and it has to be addressed. This way, everything gets explained and it propels the story further."

"By writing off two of our most popular female characters?" questioned Frieda.

"Who said anything about writing them off?" I asked.

Trip, who had yet to say anything, chortled. "This I have to hear."

"Alexis is a great actress. I may not like her on a personal level, but I don't want to get in the habit of unloading people just because they rub me the wrong way. As far as I'm concerned, both murders can go unsolved for a while. Having a character as unpredictable and dangerous as Sarah on the canvas will only help. It'll tell the audience that anything can happen in Deception Pass."

"What do you think will happen when your mother finds out you're killing her off?" Trip asked. It was clear he wanted to be in the room when she did.

"But we're not *writing* her off. Sarah's going to be a total lunatic. Certifiable. After she kills Vienna, Vienna will start appearing to her. Not as a ghost," I quickly promised. Scooter would be heartbroken. "She'll be one of the voices that crazy Sarah hears all the time. Vienna will torment Sarah with the same bad advice that she doled out when she was alive."

> VIENNA'S SPECTER
> Go ahead, Sarah. Take
> Jacqueline's jelly doughnut.
> She's too busy making time
> with your ex-boyfriend to
> notice. And while you're at
> it, smother Marco in his
> sleep.

> SARAH
> (FRAYING) No, no, no!

Trip seemed to be loving it. And why wouldn't he? Here was a chance to stick it to my mother after she cleaned him out in the divorce years ago. "So we'd never actually see her again? She'd be a disembodied voice?"

I hadn't thought of it that way, but hey, we'd save a ton of money on the costume budget.

"I admit that this is a scandalous idea," I told them, wrapping up. "But see, I was telling Richard and Mom last night over dinner that the danger in getting awards recognition is that it can make you complacent. Fat. Slow." I tossed a look at Richard, who looked like he was going to blow.

"Stupid?" he asked, quoting himself.

"Exactly. And I want this show to be the opposite. I want to push harder and faster and stronger. I want our show on the cover of all those soap rags for months to come. Can you imagine how people will react if we leak the news that we're killing Vienna one week after Mom gets her first Emmy nomination? They'll be calling for my head."

"And tuning in by the millions," said Greg. The *cha-ching* in Trip's and Frieda's heads was so loud it didn't matter that it wasn't audible.

The room was quiet for a moment. I could tell Richard's mind was racing, but I knew it was a trip to nowhere. For once, I was ahead of the curve. Far enough ahead to lap him.

And then Trip spoke up.

"Mallory, I love it. It's fantastic. And you're right, we do need to exploit this opportunity. But this isn't the way to do it."

"Excuse me?" I asked. I'd been flying so high that it hadn't occurred to me how hard the fall would be should my wings get clipped.

"This idea of yours . . . it's not *Likely Story*. It's *Good As Gold*."

"*Good As Gold* is off the air," I said.

"Exactly," said Trip. "And this is the sort of thing that got it there."

"Hold on a second." *Keep your voice down, Mallory.* "Are you saying it's too . . . soapy?"

"It's smart and it's fun, but it's regular soap. And that's not what we bought from you. Now, before you fly off the handle at me for foisting the murder plot on you, let me say: You were right all along. We should have trusted your vision for the show from the outset. But making Sarah a crazed killer? Turning Vienna into a figment of her imagination? If this was your mother's show, I'd have given you my blessing twenty minutes ago. But it's your show. And this idea seems to me like you're overcompensating for one or two misguided notes we gave you way back when we started out on this ride." He got up and buttoned his jacket. "Keep at it. I'm sure you'll think of something. Greg, give Sales a call and tell them we're back on."

Richard stopped Trip at the door. "Mallory had another idea—I'm surprised she hasn't mentioned it."

"Sum it up for me, Mal," said Trip.

Richard allowed me one interminable second of panic before throwing me a lifeline . . . only to strangle me with it. "We were batting it around last night over the dinner table, but she dropped it pretty quickly, thought you wouldn't go for it. What would you think of pairing Ryan with Vienna? Kind of a May-December thing? Two Emmy nominees together in a steamy student-teacher romance? We might get the same amount of publicity without exposing ourselves to a lot of negativity, from outside the show *and* within."

"I like it," said Trip, without a moment's pause to critique. He looked at me. "That's the type of thing you could run with. Don't be afraid to bring these ideas to me. I'm open to anything." And then they were gone, taking all the oxygen with them.

"I'd shut the door and scream at you if I thought you could take it right now," Richard said arrogantly.

"My mother and Dallas?! Have you lost your mind?!" I hissed.

"You should be down on your knees thanking me. I just credited you with a story that Trip didn't think twice about latching onto, one your mother and I came up with all on our own. That's one of the two last favors I'm going to do for you, Mallory. The other is this: I won't tell your mother about the undignified end you had planned for her."

"The better to blackmail me?"

"All I want is peace," he professed.

"Well, you're not going to get it by taking potshots at me. In fact, all you've done is inspire me to take up arms."

"Let it go, Mallory," he called as I walked out the door. "Work with us on this and you'll have another nomination this time next year."

I resisted the urge to tell him off or slam the door behind me. That would have been dishonorable. I'd made the decision to play his game, and he'd managed to outplay me.

But I was a quick study.

———

I skipped the writers' room and went straight for the parking lot. I needed to vent, but the staff would only whip me into a frenzy that might last hours. I'd have to take out my frustration on the square-dance floor. But Tamika was waiting for me by the car.

"How'd it go?" she asked.

"Let's just say I have newfound respect for Richard's skill for torture. He'd have made the Inquisition proud."

"That bad, huh?"

"I'm going to get him, Tamika. Him and my mother both."

"I don't know whether to clap my hands or hide under the bed when you talk like that. What are you going to do?"

"I'm still weighing my options. But you'll be the first to know when I settle on a plan of action."

"Okay . . . but in the interest of keeping your priorities straight—"

"Please don't tell me to live and let live. I don't think I could take it."

"Relax. I'm through giving you advice about how to deal with your mom. That woman is some kind of dastardly."

"What are you talking about? Did she go demanding a rewrite or something while I was in with Richard?"

"I kind of wish she had. Here," she said, handing me her iPhone. "Take a look."

The Web address read www.likelywhorey.com. Not a good sign. "How clever," I drawled.

"Scroll down a little," Tamika said. I did, and there it was: a splashy, full-color image of Dallas and me at the end of my driveway, very close together—*kissing-distance* close. Underneath the picture screamed a question in some incredibly

93

tacky font I'd never seen before: **Mallory does Dallas?!**

"It's linked all over the soap message boards," Tamika said, like she'd just found out the governor had denied me clemency.

He might as well have. Square dancing beckoned, and Keith was still waiting.

The way my life worked, I was sure he'd seen the post . . . and I'd have to answer for it.

"I could fill in for Scooter," offered Dallas.
The gym suddenly went quiet.

n i n e

Kimberly the Publicist texted me all the way to school, starting with

SAW SITE, AM WORKING ON IT.

It went downhill from there.

SITE OWNER UNREACHABLE.
IT'S NEWS TO DALLAS.
LAWYERS: NO GROUNDS FOR SUIT.
PEREZ HILTON SEEKS COMMENT.
ARE YOU DATING DALLAS???

I turned off my phone.

I was on time for gym by seconds, but too late by half a day to save Keith from catching wind of my mother's sneak attack. Scooter was the first to find me in the crowd. If the dirty looks from my classmates didn't provide me a damage assessment, the fluttering in Scooter's voice did.

"The cheerleaders know, and so do the theater kids. But I don't think news has trickled down to the band geeks or Model UN yet."

"I'm glad it doesn't really matter to me what any of them think," I lied. "The only person in this building I care about besides you is Keith." That was the truth.

"Well, in my professional opinion, this doesn't have to be a deal breaker. Practically the same thing happened to Geneva on *Good As Gold* when her fling with the champion matador got broadcast over the PA at the bullring. It wasn't easy, but she reclaimed her good name in the end. Okay, she had to run with the bulls to do it. But maybe a good explanation is all you need to make things right with Keith. You have one . . . right?"

"It was totally innocent, Scooter. That picture was taken completely out of context."

"Phew. I mean, that's what I assumed. Sure, it *looks* all romantic, but photos can be doctored. Just look at what happened to Geneva in 2002. . . ." Scooter's voice faded as I scanned the gym for signs of Keith. It was Friday, and Friday tended to mean his red vintage New Coke T-shirt. He liked to start the weekend off with a bang. I finally saw him sitting on the floor with part of our square, chatting it up with some girl.

Only it wasn't just some girl. It was Amelia.

"Oh, *hell* no," I muttered.

Scooter nipped at my heels as I made a beeline for my boyfriend.

"Oh, hi, Mallory," Amelia purred. "We were just talking about you. How's Dallas?"

I was itching to scratch a comeback into her, but this was

not the time to put Amelia in her place, at least not until I knew what was up with her and Keith. He couldn't look me in the eye. A sign of embarrassment, I hoped (embarrassment beat anger)—but was he embarrassed to be seen with Amelia or embarrassed to be seen with me? It was a toss-up.

"Can we talk?"

The screech of feedback drowned out Keith's answer. Coach Samson tested a mic and told the class to square up—it was time to hoe down.

Keith took up his place on my left and bowed to my curtsy as the first banjo twangs of "Billy's Hornpipe" bounced off the bleachers.

"So what's up with you and Amelia?" I asked. "Are you two friends all of a sudden?" It was a roll of the dice, but I had to know.

"Seriously? You're seriously asking me that?" Snake eyes.

"Allemande left your partner!" Coach called out.

Keith took my hand, but his grasp was limp. "Before I even get to ask you about your night with Dallas?"

"Nothing happened, Keith," I swore.

"Grand right and left!"

Keith and I joined right hands. "You believe me, right?" I asked. But he pulled by me, heading straight toward Amelia. I threaded between guys as I kept a watchful eye on my boyfriend. So much so that I nearly ran smack into Scooter.

"Promenade your partner home!"

Keith took my clammy hands and escorted me back to base.

"Maybe this isn't the best time to talk," I said.

"When is it a good time, Mallory? Not yesterday, when I

wanted to take you out to celebrate and you told me you were too busy with a 'work thing'"—he gave it air quotes—"conveniently forgetting to mention that Dallas was going to be there. And it wasn't a good time when I gave you a chance to come clean this morning."

I wanted to call him on this—on testing me instead of coming out and asking me about it when he'd found out Dallas had been over—but there were degrees of wrong in this situation, and I knew that mine was much greater.

"I just mean that it's hard to have a conversation when we're dancing around to fiddle music."

"Grand Square!"

"I want to explain. And I want to say I'm sorry. Can we get out of here? Please."

His moment's hesitation caused a pileup as Amelia, Scooter, and the other two couples, expecting room where there was none, jostled and cramped each other. Our square folded in on itself, and Amelia leveled us with a disapproving look. "Come on," I told Keith. "They can make do with a triangle for a while."

The nearest empty space was the boys' locker room. Not the stuff of fantasies—at least, not mine—but there was some privacy, and no immediate threat of patrolling teachers.

Keith sat on a bench, then leaned against a locker. We'd had our share of confrontations, but it never got any easier.

"I should have told you what the situation was last night," I said flat out. "I thought you'd get mad."

"You thought right."

"I guess I was going to lose either way."

"Maybe. Only, the other way doesn't end in you and

Dallas doing whatever it was you were doing at the end of your driveway last night."

"It was nothing! It wasn't even a hug. He was just being nice. After my mom and Richard were total jerks."

"I'm the boyfriend! It's my job to be nice. I feel like an idiot standing here arguing with you about whether it's okay for another guy to be your friend, but it's not the first time we've had this conversation about the same thing, with the same guy."

I thought this was particularly unfair, seeing as how I'd patiently acted as "the other woman" when Keith and I first started going out. His ex-girlfriend—the one he'd cheated on with me for months—was probably a big fan of LikelyWhorey.com.

"And now I'm getting e-mails from all kinds of people I've never heard of who want to know if we broke up or if I'm dumping you or if I'm going to fight Dallas. This isn't what I signed up for."

"Right. You signed up for a pushover who didn't mind being second best while you canoodled with another girl." I couldn't help it—the irony of the situation had to be pointed out.

"So you get a free pass to play around with Dallas because of everything with Erika?"

"For the last time, I'm not *playing around* with Dallas. Unlike how you were playing around with me when Erika was still calling you her boyfriend. What I'm saying is, you don't get a free pass to make all kinds of assumptions just because the shoe is now on the other foot. If you feel guilty and paranoid, it's because you cheated on Erika, not me."

Keith was trembling, pissed. "It takes two people to cheat,

Mallory. If you didn't like the situation, you didn't have to be a part of it."

"Well, what about the situation we're in right now? Do you want out of this one?"

"Do you think I'd be standing here yelling if I did?"

It was as true as it was startling. Keith was the model of serenity, but here he was, testing out the limits of his larynx. And so was I. I tried to remember a time before *Likely Story* that I yelled, and I came up short. I wondered how much of the rest of my life could be divided up that way: Before *Likely Story* and After.

"I'm sorry," I said again, this time with new meaning. Or real meaning. "I feel like I've been making one mistake after another for the past two days. I can't get anything right. And now I have some anonymous Web site calling me a slut."

"It's okay. And you're not," he told me, pulling me into an embrace. I usually settled so comfortably into a nook against his chest. But the fit now felt off.

"I should've been more understanding," said Keith.

"I should've been honest with you," I said.

"I should've broken up with Erika right from the start."

"I should've tried harder to make you and Dallas friends."

"Let's not get crazy, okay?"

We heard the sound of a flush from around a couple of corners. We flinched, realizing we'd had a spectator. And not just any spectator. The kind that got off on misery.

"You guys sure have a flair for the dramatic," Amelia's brother, Jake, said as he appeared around the corner. "Why don't you give Keith a part on your show, Mallory? Oops, silly me, I already know why. 'Cause then you'd have to take it away from him and give it to someone else."

"Do you just sit on the can all day hoping for the chance to eavesdrop on people?"

"No, but if there's a chance I'll ever hear something as spicy as what I just heard, maybe I will. I would've cleared my throat or farted extra loud or something, but I didn't want to interrupt. I'm glad I didn't, either. You two put on a good show. Is there more to come? Or is it over?"

Keith put his arm around me and we walked out together, but Jake's question rang in my ears. I wasn't sure I knew the answer. I wasn't sure Keith knew, either.

"You must know by now that you can't live in both worlds. You have to choose eventually."

ten

Keith tried to get out of his shift at California Pizza Kitchen, but nobody was willing to give up a free Friday night. We made a point of agreeing about how much it sucked to be us, but I was secretly relieved and wouldn't have been surprised if he was, too. I'd been sapped by the events of the day. Being around Keith for much longer might have been work when it should have been play.

I had my studio-provided driver stop my car half in, half out of the driveway. I could see the spot where Dallas and I talked the night before. I thought about my mother. It would have been easy to blame her for the picture and the Web site but impossible to explain it. I couldn't see how humiliating me *and* Dallas *and* Keith would benefit her. Any stalker fan or desperate paparazzo could have been lurking in the rosebushes, waiting for just the right moment to snap just the wrong picture. It didn't matter who'd done it, just that it was done. I'd officially joined the ranks of the fair game.

The intercom at the gate crackled to life, and Mom's voice

yanked me from my reverie. "Mallory, don't just sit there brooding. Come inside."

"What for? Have you got some of your typically jaded advice to dole out? How to survive a sex scandal?" I felt like I was at a drive-thru, getting my licks in to go.

"Leave the soap at the studio, darling. I just want to make sure you're all right." Suddenly I could see how Trip would have found Vienna's voice-over appealing. There was something almost human in my mother's choice of words, and vaguely sensitive in her tone. Had she been saying this in person, though, her facial expression would have given away just how little she really cared. "Look on the bright side—it was a very good picture."

"My boyfriend would disagree."

"Well, what do you expect? Kevin's not showbiz. You should be proud of yourself. Your very first nasty gossip item is a rite of passage. We'll commemorate it with a party, just the two of us." I wasn't sure, but what she was suggesting sounded a little like *bonding*. Then she added, "And we can talk about your new story for Ryan and Vienna."

Sucker punched, I asked the driver to put the car in reverse. "Sorry, Mom. I'm not in the mood to celebrate."

Trekking the 405 over the hill through Friday night traffic would test the patience of Job, but I had KCRW to keep me company in the backseat, and the promise that my destination was worth the wait. Things always seemed a little less life-or-death after a visit to Gina's house in Tarzana.

A clot of cars was parked in front. I didn't want to intrude when she had company, and I was all but resigned to facing the music at home, when a glint of chrome beckoned from between two cars. When the driver pulled up a bit farther, I saw it: a gleaming motorcycle leaning against its kickstand all sultry-like, its handlebars cocked like arms crossed in front of itself. If this thing could talk, it would have said, *He's inside. Got a light?*

Before, I'd been seeking refuge. Now I was seeking answers. What was Dallas doing at Gina's? And who else did she have over?

Whoever it was, they were having a good time. When Gina answered the door, she let the sound of laughter rush out behind her.

"Mallory!" The great thing about Gina was that she was always happy to see me.

"Hi, Gina."

"You're here!"

"I am."

"I thought you were the pizza guy."

"I get that a lot."

Usually by this point in my visit, I'd be halfway down the hall on my way to the fridge, but Gina made no move to invite me in.

"It's a bad time, isn't it? I should've called."

This snapped her out of whatever trance my surprise arrival had put her in.

"Nonsense, it's never a bad time for you," she said, welcoming me in. "I heard all about that nasty Web site. You must be livid."

"It hasn't been a fun forty-eight hours."

"Come on in and put your feet up—we'll have you forgetting all about that in no time. Hey, guys, *Mallory's* here."

The mix of voices went silent as Gina escorted me inside. Dallas, Francesca, Javier, and Greg were all seated around the table, which was piled with poker chips, cards, and (for those who were drinking age) beer. They couldn't have looked more frightened if I'd found them all in the buff.

"Relax, guys," I said. "I totally couldn't hear you talking about me."

Javier and Greg tittered nervously as Francesca hugged me. "We've been sitting here worrying up a storm about you."

"And figuring out how to avenge you," Javier added.

"Let me know if you have any ideas," I told them.

Dallas had gotten up but was keeping his distance. Francesca chided him. "Nobody's taking pictures in here, Dallas—it's okay to hug her."

Still, he didn't approach. "I wanted to call you but thought you'd be out with Keith tonight. I figured the last thing you two needed was my popping up on your caller ID."

"Good thinking. We're okay, by the way. Keith and me." I could feel the rest of the room wondering whether they should wait us out or talk among themselves.

"I knew you would be. Keith's a good guy. I bet he brushed the whole thing off."

"Close. I hope your mother didn't call and say 'Don't you wish you were in gross anatomy class right now?' "

"She didn't, but if she does, I'll just nod my head and tell her she was right all along." He smiled. I did, too.

"You play poker, Mallory?" asked Greg, right on time.

"Texas hold 'em. Amelia taught me."

Everyone booed Amelia's name as Dallas told me I'd just happened on their supersecret monthly poker game. "And by 'secret,' we mean 'Don't tell Alexis,' " said Francesca.

"She won't hear about it from me."

"Good." Francesca pushed the bowl of pretzels my way. "Pull up a chair."

"What's the ante? I've got all of five dollars and a coupon for a free Jamba Juice."

Javier leaned in. "We don't play for money, babe. We play for secrets."

This could be trouble.

But it was the kind of trouble I could get into.

It was quickly explained to me that Dallas and Francesca had first come up with Blurt Poker as a team-building exercise back in New York at Juilliard. There had been some tension over the non-traditional casting of their third-year production of *Suddenly, Last Summer* (Francesca as Dr. Cukrowicz and Dallas as Mrs. Violet Venable). Francesca suggested that it might be harder to resent each other if they were privy to each other's dirty little secrets—all the terrible little things that made them who they were. I wasn't sure the logic behind this was that sound. But factor in that actors are, as a rule, over-sharers, and it made more sense. Their rules had apparently been working for a while, so I kept my reservations to myself . . . even when I was asked to cough up something to ante in.

"How do I know if my secret is on par with everyone else's?"

"You don't have to break the bank on the first round," said Gina. "You'll pick it up as we go."

"Okay . . ." I went with the first thing that came to mind. "I'm a homewrecker. Is that enough to start?"

"Girl means business," Francesca marveled.

Greg dealt.

Things I learned that night (mostly because I was a severely underestimated poker player):

- Gina's in night school, getting a degree in psychology.
- Greg's film school friends call him a sellout.
- Javier kept his job as an assistant manager at Urban Outfitters for two months into production of *Likely Story*. "Who here didn't think we were going to flop?"
- Francesca told Richard about Dallas's motorcycle in exchange for her pick of dressing rooms.
- Richard told Dallas he could keep his motorcycle if he promised to attend my mom's wedding. "Do any of us really see that wedding happening?"
- Gina turned down a makeup job in 1976 because she thought it was a little "out-there." In 1977 that project hit theaters: *Star Wars*.
- Greg's okay with being called a sellout, but it scares him that that doesn't scare him. "In five years, when my friends are still waiting tables in Silverlake, I'll be VP of Programming. If that makes me a bad person, I'll leave—but I don't think the job in itself will make me a bad person."
- Javier had taken to anonymously posting raves of his performance on his own fan Web site. "That makes me a worse person than Greg."
- Francesca wasn't surprised that she hadn't been

nominated for an Emmy . . . but she did want one. However, she wanted Alexis's failure to be nominated even more. "So I consider that a win."

• Dallas has an Emmy speech already written, and it mortifies him that he does. "It's the same for the Obies and the Tonys, with a few tweaks," he said.

• Gina has no one to take to the ceremony.

• Neither does Greg.

• Francesca hasn't had one date since she moved to LA. In fact, she's had negative-one dates. "We get to my door, but instead of trying to kiss me good night, he asks if I can get his head shot to the casting director."

• Javier had a −1 date with the same guy.

Dallas won that hand.

Things I divulged:

• Richard had taken to wearing a smoking jacket around the house. No, he hadn't started smoking.

• I cheated every year on the President's Physical Fitness Test.

• The last time she was at my house, Amelia left her favorite vintage purse. I kicked it under my bed after our big fight and it hadn't moved from there since.

• Amelia's brother, Jake, kissed me.

Thing I was interested in learning: Who was Dallas bringing to the Emmys?

Things I was not interested in divulging: anything involving Keith.

Everybody folded but me and Dallas. "Look at the size of that pot," said Javier. A mound of red chips was spread over the table. "Whoever loses has got to give up something juicy," he singsonged.

"I'm not sure I have anything juicy left to tell," I joked, prompting a round of guffaws. "But . . . I'll see your secret and raise you mine." I threw in a bunch of chips.

"It had better be good, Mallory," Francesca cautioned. "I happen to know Dallas has a few doozies left up his sleeve."

"That's what I'm banking on."

"Shut up, Francesca, or maybe my secret will be that I know *yours*." Dallas saw my bet and raised me.

"I don't think so. I think you can do better than that." I matched and upped the ante.

"Wouldn't you like to know?" He didn't back down.

"Not only would I like to know, I think I am going to know in just a minute."

"Big talker."

"Hey, I'm putting my money where my mouth is. You think I can't back it up?"

Chips were spilling off the pile, practically into our laps.

"Go ahead and call if you're so sure," I challenged, training my eyes right at his. Dallas didn't break my gaze. "You could always fold," I offered. Dallas pushed his remaining chips into the middle of the table.

"I'm all in. It's your call, Mallory."

I considered my options. Backing down wasn't one of them.

"Call."

I flipped over my cards.

"A pair of fives?" cried Gina. "You were bluffing?!"

I began to scoop up my winnings. "Bluffing is my way of life."

"Not so fast, Tex." Dallas revealed his hand: a straight. I was laid low.

Dallas accepted congratulations and told me to 'fess up.

"And make it good," he added.

I bit my lip. There were some secrets that were really not meant for sharing . . . but there were some that might do a lot of good if told to the right people.

"Are you sure you want to know, Dallas? It's about you."

Four pairs of eyes darted from me to him. Dallas's usually steady smile visibly quivered.

"Now I want to know," said Francesca.

"Be careful, Mallory," Greg whispered.

"Come on!" Javier bellowed.

Dallas swallowed. "Why don't we call it even?"

I shook my head. "No way. Fair's fair."

"But this is your first time. You shouldn't have to tell something you're not ready to."

Somewhere in the back of my mind, this raised a red flag, like he had an idea of what I might say. If he did, he was wrong. But I did wonder what he was thinking.

"I knew what I signed up for. Don't worry—I won't embarrass you any more than I already have. It goes like this.

Mom and Richard want me to write a story where Ryan and Vienna have an affair."

I expected wretching. I expected outrage.

I got oohs and aahs.

"Omigod! Does this mean I'd get to have all kinds of blowout scenes with your mom?" begged Francesca.

"Forget the Emmy, Fran. Slap Vienna, and you'd get the Purple Heart!" Javier proclaimed.

Gina knew better than to come down on one side or another. "Your mother's certainly a big fan of Ryan's. She'd love it."

I looked to Dallas, hoping he'd know from the expression on my face that I thought it was a crime against nature.

"It's a little out of left field, isn't it?" he said. This was a start.

"Exactly. Ryan is in love with Jacqueline. End of story."

"But he doesn't really know what his feelings are," Francesca countered. "He's totally ripe for manipulating. This would be the perfect time for a man-eater like Vienna to gobble him up."

"She has a point," Dallas said. He looked at me and shrugged. "It could be fun."

"And sexy," said Javier.

"And dramatic," said Francesca.

And a complete disaster. I was not going to write love scenes for Dallas and my mother. She'd taken my show. I wasn't going to let her take Dallas, too.

That was one secret I couldn't let slip. But when I looked at Greg, I saw that he understood.

"You're not crazy," he said to me once the actors' conversation had moved on to two cameramen who'd recently fallen in love over star filters and light-meter readings. "It's a stupid, stupid idea."

"Thanks," I told him.

"Seriously. It's not your feelings for, um, the actors involved that's telling you to stop this. It's your feelings about the show."

"It's so hard to tell the difference nowadays," I confessed.

"Try. I know you can do it."

That made one of us.

"*I've seen men have all kinds of effects on my mother,
but I've never seen one make her molt.*"

e l e v e n

By the time I left the game, even Gina had been swept up in all the "Ryenna" talk. I told myself that Greg was right—they didn't know what they were talking about. They weren't my target audience. I was. I was writing for a nation of Mallorys.

So when I got home, I evaded the dastardly duo and fired up my laptop. Final Draft's blinking cursor dared me to give it a shot. It was better than logging on to www.likelywhorey.com or sifting through typo-riddled rants from Alexis's fan club president . . . but not by much.

> (INT., VIENNA'S OFFICE)
> VIENNA sits at her desk,
> eraser end of a pencil poised
> flirtatiously at her lips.
> RYAN sits opposite, jumpy.
>
> VIENNA
> . . .

RYAN

. . .

VIENNA

I can sit here all day.

RYAN

Not me. I've got places to be.

VIENNA

Waves to surf? Hearts to
break?

RYAN

(GETS UP TO GO) Kid sisters
to babysit.

VIENNA

Making a pit stop at your
dealer's place first? (RYAN
STOPS) That's right. I know
all about the monkey on your
back. Don't look so surprised;
I'm a guidance counselor,
remember? I know things.

RYAN

I just wish you knew when
to quit.

                    VIENNA
        I'm too stubborn for that.
        (CLOSE TO HIM) You're dying
        for a fix, aren't you? (LOCKS
           THE DOOR) Well, I'm not
         letting you out of here.

                     RYAN
         You're crazy! Let me out!

                    VIENNA
        Not going to happen. You're going
        to detox right here in this room.
        And I'm going to help you do it!
        (SHE PULLS HIM CLOSE TO HER AND
        KISSES HIM PASSIONATELY) Mallory,
          you might have an easier time
         comprehending this story if you
        wrote me like a real human being.

                   MALLORY
                 Excuse me?

                     RYAN
             She's got a point.

                    VIENNA
          Who tries to kiss a person
          out of a drug addiction?

                     123

                         RYAN
                    No one I know.

                        MALLORY
                 They wanted Ryan/Vienna?
                 Here's Ryan/Vienna.

                        VIENNA
                 No, this is Ryan and your
                  caricature of a campy,
                 predatory cougar. You're
                 better than this, Mallory.
                  But you're too caught up
                  hating your mother to
                     realize it.

I passed the pages to Tamika during Monday morning's production meeting. She pulled me aside later and felt my forehead for a fever.

"How often do you write yourself into scenes?" she asked.

"I'm taking the Fifth on that one. Forget about the pages
and just tell me what you think of the idea. Is Richard on to
something? Or will he destroy us all?"

She didn't have to open her mouth to give me an answer.

"Oh my God. You love it."

"It's pure soap," she said, apologetic. "And you of all people should know that. The thing is—and this is an important
thing—it's definitely been done a million thousand times before, and the whole point of this show is to go new places. So

                         124

while my *Good As Gold*–loving soul would love a strong dose of unexpected seduction, I also know it's not necessarily the show you're trying to give us. Look—are you sure you're feeling okay?"

I didn't know what I was feeling, but I knew it was far from okay.

"Maybe you should tell me exactly why *you* hate the idea so much. Besides the fact that it's the demon brainchild of your mother and Richard."

Could I tell her that what it boiled down to was that the image of my mother lusting after Dallas knotted my stomach? And if so, would I have to explain to her—or myself—why it did?

"I don't know. It just feels wrong."

"I love you, but you're going to have to do better than that if you want to kill the story."

She was right. Putting my foot down would be meaningless if I couldn't hold my ground.

Lunch that day was on *Soap Opera Summary*. Kimberly Winters had pitched their editors an informal press conference to dish about the Emmys. Richard, Mom, Dallas, and I were scheduled to sit around a table on set and be charming as we talked over limp Caesar salads. Given my missteps lately, I figured I'd just keep my mouth shut and try not to get in the way. Kimberly told me not to worry. "Expect fawning," she said. "But I'll be there to steer the conversation, just in case. They'll be on the lookout for anything sensational they can smear across the cover."

Alexis caught me on my way to the studio floor. I tried to beg off, but she snagged my wrist and held on like a hyena grabbing a carcass.

"Tell me something's being done about that awful Web site." Her faux concern was underwhelming.

"Would if we could, but we can't, so we won't cry over it."

"That's terrible. Hiding out and taking pictures of you? Making trouble for your boyfriend? That sort of thing should be a crime."

"It is. They call it stalking."

"Well, I hope they catch whoever's responsible. Somebody needs to make it safe for people like us to go out in public."

"It hasn't stopped me yet. Somehow I doubt it would stop you, either."

"Naturally. And while we're on the subject, I'd love for you to participate in a charity event I'm organizing." She handed me a flyer. "The cast and crew of *Likely Story* versus the cast and crew of *Tropical Hospital* in a friendly softball match to benefit research into pediatric cancer."

Hmm. Perhaps Alexis did indeed have a heart where I'd previously envisioned a breeding ball of snakes.

"I know you're not really a 'gym' person, but we could always use a mascot."

Or maybe not.

"I'll bring my glove and everything," I said. "Slow pitch or fast pitch?"

She had no idea what I was talking about.

"Let me know when you figure it out," I told her.

"Friends and family are invited, too," she called. "Bring Keith! Or whoever you're with these days!"

By the time I made it down to the floor, the choicest seats were taken, forcing me to paste on a smile and sit next to Richard. Dallas was trapped between Mom and Marilyn Kinsey from *SOS*, who was already dishing out questions about where he'd put his Emmy if he won.

Kimberly was true to her word. The soap journos stuck to agreed-upon subjects and we toed the party line.

What do you think about the nominations? "Why, we're pleased as punch, if puzzled that the rest of our fabulous cast didn't get nominated."

What do you think about your chances? "We're just happy to be here."

How would winning awards change the show? "We don't make the show to get awards, we make the show for the fans. We love you, fans!"

How does it feel to be nominated for the first time in your (looong) career, not as Geneva, the character you're best known for, but as Vienna? "You know, I feel a real affinity for Vienna. She wields a mighty empathy for those around her. She *feels* with a depth that Geneva could never have mined. I don't think Geneva was ever deserving of an Emmy. Vienna, though, is another matter."

Is there enough room in the Hayden household for three Emmys? "My, but I have a whole room set aside for them!"

Only my mother could take that question seriously.

What's next for the citizens of Deception Pass? Can fans of Likely Story expect big shake-ups anytime soon?

The question had been directed at me, but Richard cut me off. "I think I can field this one," he said.

I felt the hair on the back of my neck rise, and I realized: *I have hair on the back of my neck.*

"Do you mind?" he asked, like he was giving me the choice.

"Go right ahead," I said, ever the obedient writer and stepdaughter-to-be.

"While we're very excited about the prospect of bringing home some trophies next month, we've always got our eyes on the story."

Mom rang in. "That's what we're about. We're storytellers, first and foremost."

"We've got a number of big stories already building to a climax," Richard added. "The most interesting one, to my mind, is Ryan and Jacqueline's romance."

"Aren't they great?" Mom encouraged. "Everyone just loves Dallas."

"Just doing my job," Dallas said.

Richard went on. "And doing a mesmerizing job of it. It's had us thinking that we've been pretty unfair to the rest of the cast, overinvolving Ryan in this one plot."

"Spread the wealth, that's what I always say," said my mother, who'd never before said or thought that in her life.

"Which is why we've come up with an incredible twist to the Ryan/Jacqueline story that I'd like to reveal exclusively to you—"

This had gone too far. "Richard," I interrupted, "I'm not sure the timing is right to be talking about this particular story."

Richard laughed. "Mallory is an incredibly talented writer, but like any writer, she's got neuroses up the wazoo. She's always saying her work is never good enough."

"You should hear what I think of *your* work."

If he wouldn't take my hints, I'd have to force them down his throat.

Richard ignored me and leaned in, taking the editors into his confidence. "Ryan and Jacqueline are going to find a little fly in the ointment," he said, taking Mom's hand. "A sexy little fly by the name of Vienna."

Marilyn Kinsey nearly fell out of her chair. If she'd been wearing pearls, she'd have been clutching them. "Ryan and Vienna are going to have an affair?!"

Mom pressed onward as I tried hard not to hyperventilate. "Vienna is going to find herself desperately attracted to Ryan, in a way she's never been attracted to a person before. And once she realizes that, she's going to fight tooth and nail for his love."

Marilyn, who was of my mother's generation, fluttered with excitement. "A May-December romance with two of daytime's hottest stars! Sign me up!"

The rest of the editors buzzed with questions. I caught Dallas's eye from across the table. He looked worried. Worried for me.

Someone asked how I felt about writing a sex scene for my mother and Dallas. Mom must have known by the steam coming out of my nostrils that I wasn't happy about it, and she spoke up before I could choose just the right curse word.

"Are you kidding? You saw that Web site, didn't you? The one with the picture of Mallory and Dallas? She just wishes she was writing that sex scene for herself!"

She meant it as a joke. And like a lot of the worst, most hurtful jokes ever made, it was made at the expense of more than just one person. In that moment, I could see the headline item of Internet celebrity news cycles for days to come: SOAP MOM SAYS DAUGHTER'S HOT FOR CO-STAR! Worse still, in that moment, I could see Keith's reaction.

Dallas scrambled to make it better. "Mallory and I are just friends. She has a boyfriend." I gave him points for trying, but that didn't really make it better. Mom joined in, perhaps because she noticed the suddenly throbbing vein on my forehead, perhaps because she didn't want to sleep with one eye open for the rest of her life.

"But who wouldn't want to write themselves into a sex scene with this sensitive young hunk?" she purred.

I forced myself to slow down my breathing. There was only one thing left to do. Fortunately, it was one of the things I got paid to do.

Rewrite.

"The thing is," I said slowly, choosing my words carefully, "Richard's only told you half of the story."

Marilyn—who gulped down spoilers like my mother gulped Grey Goose—was instantly hooked, lined, and sinkered. "What do you mean?" she asked with breathless anticipation.

It was one thing to hear a story from Richard. But now it was the Future of Soaps talking. I had to make it good. "I can only tell you if everyone here promises that this next bit goes unpublished for a while," I said coyly. "I promise not to spill it to anyone else, and I'll personally call and let you know when it's all right to run with it."

The editors nodded in unison.

Richard was uneasy—and rightly so, the big jerk. "I'm

thinking you're right, Mallory," he said. "Maybe we should hold off on telling all."

"Trust me, Richard. And trust the good people at *Soap Opera Summary*. They've given us their word. No way are they going to tell anyone that right before Vienna succeeds in seducing Ryan, she discovers the horrible secret that could destroy them both . . . that he's her long-lost son."

Everyone in the room—even Dallas, even Mom—gasped.

Everyone but Richard, who was busy swallowing his tongue.

There was no going back now.

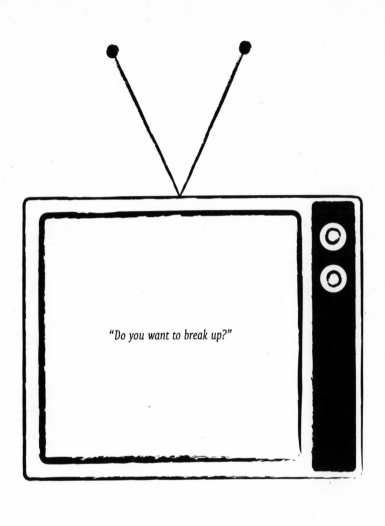

twelve

"I've HAD it with you!" Richard screamed.

We were behind closed doors in his office. But at the volume he was hitting, all the assistants in the production office outside could hear him. I didn't really care.

"Where do you get off undermining me that way?!" he went on.

I tried to contain my grin. Then I thought, *Why contain it?*

"Doesn't feel too good, being treated with disrespect, does it?"

"I am the *executive producer,* Mallory. I am your boss."

"And Trip Carver is *your* boss. Shall I get him on the line and let him know about the little end run you just tried to pull on me?"

"Trip signed off on Ryan/Vienna, right here in this office, right here in front of you."

"He was on his way out the door, Richard. He was hardly listening. He'd have liked an idea about Mom playing Vienna's twin brother. And you know something? I might have liked your idea, too, if only you'd given me a chance to sit with it and come around. Couldn't you have waited a few weeks? Couldn't you have talked it over with me and let me brainstorm it with my staff?"

"Who are you trying to kid? You'd never have written that story without me lighting the fire. You can't stand to see your mother enjoy any kind of success."

"Not when it comes at my expense!"

"This was a good story, Mallory. It was good for Dallas, it was good for your mother, and it was good for the show. Now you've ruined it. Best case scenario, *Summary* keeps its word and doesn't spoil the story. Best case scenario, your mother doesn't look like such a fool that Emmy voters can't take her seriously. But if they do let this plot idea slip, she'll be the laughingstock of the industry. She'll be a soap opera cliché *again,* and it will be at her own daughter's hands. She's wanted this award more than anything for decades, but no one will vote for a woman who doesn't even have her daughter's support."

"Remind me, Richard—who exactly wrote the scripts that she got nominated for? Did I miss something? Did the little soap-opera-writing elves come into the workshop while I was asleep and write those episodes?"

"Fair enough," Richard conceded. "But that was the nomination. She needs you now for the win."

"Then she's got *a lot* of groveling to do. Especially after her little 'Mallory can't sleep with Dallas, so I will!' display in the interview. If she loses the Emmy, maybe she'll take home the Sketchy Mom of the Year Award."

"Couldn't you, just this once, do something nice for her?"

If I thought she had it in her to do the same for me, then

yes, I would have. If I thought for one second that she wouldn't throw me under a bus to get that stupid award, then yes, I would have. But this was my mother we were talking about, and she'd burned me one too many times. With the comment about Dallas, she'd crossed from first degree straight to third degree.

Now it was her turn to feel the heat.

If it had been up to Richard, I probably would have been chained to my desk until I'd found a way to make it acceptable for Vienna to luv her long-lost son. But I had to get to school—gym class beckoned.

And lo and behold, I was the undisputed queen of square dancing that day.

My do-si-dos were flawless. My courtesy turns: perfect. I square-danced with abandon, fed by loads of angry energy.

"You are truly fierce today," Scooter whispered, courtesy-turning me back to Keith with flair.

"Who *are* you?" Keith laughed as I led a star promenade with such heavenly form as to rate kudos from Coach Samson, who told us, "You keep that up and y'all are gonna have a champion square at the square-off next week!"

Maybe I went a little overboard. Amelia complained that I squeezed her hand so hard on the two-ladies chain that I broke a nail.

I didn't care. For the first time since the Emmys had reared their golden heads, I felt empowered. Like what happened to *Likely Story* was not beyond my control. Like I had a say in what happened, and that my say was loud.

———

Pinned against his Mustang in the school parking lot, I kissed Keith into submission. Not that he was fighting it.

"We never got around to celebrating," I told him. "Any-place you need to be?"

"I'll tell you, but be warned . . . the cheese factor is pretty high."

"I don't think I need to remind you that I write a soap opera. Cheese is in my blood."

"The only place I need to be is with you, Robin."

I finally traded in my rain check. We braved the Pacific Coast Highway and crawled to Malibu, picking up a bucket of steamed clams at Gladstone's on the way. By the time the sun had set over the water, we were curling our toes in the sand, busting shells, and taking in the sky.

"Over there, where the clouds meet the yellow and the or-ange?" I said, pointing it out. "That's cornfield, saffron . . . and meteor. To the layman, that smidge over there is purple. But really, it's disco."

"No such color," Keith said.

"Are you with the World Association of Color Keepers or something?"

"You got me. I'm an agent of WACK and I'm here to keep you in line."

I bumped my shoulder to his. "Thank God."

He bumped back. "So when are you going to tell me what's up with you today?"

"Does it matter?"

"I like to know what makes my girl so happy. I want to make sure it happens on a daily basis."

"I don't think this is a day I ever want to repeat. Except for this part, obviously."

I told Keith the whole story, good news first, then the backstory.

"I mean, can you imagine Dallas and my mother rolling around on a water bed? Because you know that's my mother's idea of soap romance. It has to be wet."

Keith sucked Mocha Frappuccino through a straw. "What did everyone else think about it?"

"Are you kidding? They couldn't believe I'd turned the tables on Richard."

"Not about that. I mean, the story. About Ryan and Vienna."

"Some people didn't spontaneously combust when they heard it."

"Like who?"

"Why does it matter?"

Keith shrugged. "I'm just curious. Should I not ask questions?"

Not this kind, I thought. "Well, Javier, of course. But you could put a feather boa on a pig and he'd call it genius."

"Just Javier?"

"No, not just Javier," I said, exasperated. "Francesca thought there might be something to it. And Gina, although she'd been drinking." I stopped for a second, then remembered: Less than full disclosure had gotten me into my last mess with Keith. *Suck it up, Mallory.* "And Dallas, too. But he might have been going along with everyone else. I'm not sure."

Keith went quiet.

"Does that bug you or something?" I asked.

"It just seems weird to me that all of those people plus Dallas thought it was a cool idea, but you went so far to kill it."

Had we driven through a wormhole to Opposite Land? Why was Keith siding with my mother?

"Are you on Richard's payroll or something?" I had to ask.

"I'm just saying, look at all the trouble you're in with Richard and the network people. Not to mention all the other people who are probably questioning your judgment right now. It seems like you just made problems for yourself that you could have avoided if you'd just done the story."

"Did I not explain the part about the hijacking? Or that my mom basically implied to a room full of scandalmongers that I'm into Dallas?"

Keith darkened. "Believe me, I got that part."

"Then why are we arguing? I didn't just do it for the show, I did it for us." Even though a part of me was now wondering why I'd bothered. "And for the record, Greg thought it was the stupidest idea ever, and Tamika liked the idea for another soap, but not ours. Would *you* tune in to watch my mother make out with Dallas?"

"Ew. No."

Keith sighed and looked out at the ocean for a moment. A couple of kiteboarders skipped along the water. I wished I knew how two people could be so happy when two other people were so miserable nearby.

Keith took my hand. "I'm sorry. It's your show. You know best. I'm glad you were thinking of us. It means a lot to me."

I squeezed back. But the moment was gone, and we both knew it.

Once again, the show had managed to get between us.

140

"I've done nothing to be sorry for. Unless making sacrifices for my daughter is something to be ashamed of, in which case I'm the sorriest woman alive."

t h i r t e e n

When I got home, I couldn't help but check out LikelyWhorey
.com to see what the latest rumors were.

The good news: Nobody had leaked the new storyline.

The bad news:

TO: Tips (tips@likelywhorey.com)
FROM: A Little Birdie (truthaboutmhayden@omail.com)
SUBJECT: Something rotten . . .

Ever wonder why Alexis Randall didn't get an Emmy nomination
for her portrayal of Sarah?
Ever wonder why she went from being described by the mags as
"one of the young stars of Likely Story" to being called
"increasingly pointless"?
Ever wonder why there are fewer and fewer spoilers for Sarah in
Soap Opera Summary? Why Sarah's love triangle with Dallas and
Jacqueline bit the dust so quickly? Why her screen time has all but
dried up?
Two words: . . .

"Mallory Hayden."

I slammed my laptop shut and turned to see my mother leaning in the doorway, examining a good citizenship award I'd won in second grade. Ice cubes clinked in a tumbler of vodka . . . two hundred proof. "Gina never liked your name, did you know that? She never said so, but I could tell she hated it. What can I say? Your father and I thought it so apt. . . ."

Whoa. Drunk enough to mention my father. I should've told her to go to bed, but I couldn't resist. . . . Story of my life.

"My father wanted to name me Mallory?"

She was already sloshing on to something else. "Working on some more supersecret plots? Dreaming up a whole orphanage of illegitimate children with which to weigh me down? Going to give me *a grandchild* now?"

"That *would* be piling on."

"Since when has that ever stopped anyone?" She was looking around my room like she'd landed on the surface of the moon.

"Is there something I can do for you?" I asked.

She burst out laughing. She laughed so hard she doubled over. So hard she spilled her drink. So hard that she didn't care that she'd spilled her drink!

"That's a good one, Mallory. No, I think you've done enough already." She turned to go.

"Then why did you come in here?"

"I can't recall."

"Isn't Richard with you?"

She fell a little at that one.

"Richard—my darling Richard—wanted me to get some *rest.*"

There were so many things I could've asked—like, did she really love him? Or did she just love the way he loved her?

But how could I ask those things? I'd tried once, when Mom was marrying Trip.

"It's none of your business," she'd snapped at me.

And I'd snapped right back at her, saying, "Is that what marriage is to you—*business*?" I'd felt awful for weeks afterward.

But now I couldn't feel anything. Maybe a little sad that it had come to this, but that was all.

"You should get some rest," I suggested gently.

"You know what?" she said, pointing at me. "You're right."

She started to leave, and I said, "Wait." She stopped, and I asked, "Why didn't Gina like my name?"

She raised her glass to me. "Because I told her what it meant. Didn't you ever look it up? It comes from the French. For *unlucky*." She took a swig. "Oh, now I remember. I just wanted to say good night." With that, she walked out.

I opened my laptop and looked back at the screen.

Work was going to be *really* fun tomorrow.

I took the long way to the writers' room the next morning, strolling by Richard's office. Shouts were audible from down the hall, even with the door closed. *Richard really ought to get that room soundproofed,* I thought as I approached the door.

Richard's assistant jittered, saying, "He's in there with someone!"

"I'll knock first," I promised. But I didn't get the chance. The door swung open, and I heard Richard say, "Would you please come back in here so we can figure this out together?"

Obscuring my view of Richard was my mother, though I had to look twice to be sure. She was covered head to toe in feathers.

"What are you looking at?!" she coughed.

"I didn't know the loon was native to LA."

She looked back at Richard and squawked, "I don't care how you do it. Just get it done. If I get one more call from TMZ asking for my comment, I might have to tell Trip you're in over your head." She walked off, waving at the feathers floating from her hair. I turned to Richard, who looked half rattled, half impressed.

"I've seen men have all kinds of effects on my mother, but I've never seen one make her molt."

Richard jerked a thumb at his computer screen. "Have you seen LikelyWhorey this morning?"

"Hold on a second. My mother just walked out of here trailing feathers, and you want to talk about gossip? What just happened?"

"Alexis attacked your mother with a pillow after she saw this."

I scanned the screen—and saw the same thing I'd seen last night. At top was a still from a *Likely Story* publicity shoot featuring Alexis, all smiles and girl-next-door. Beneath the photo was a blurb:

Betrayed!

That high-pitched whine you're hearing? It's the sound of the bomb we're dropping! Turns out Keith and Dallas aren't the only two people paying for Hayden family issues these days. It seems Alexis Randall's chances of getting an Emmy nomination this year were torpedoed by a close "friend" and castmate. If only she hadn't relied on that backstabber's advice when deciding what material to submit to the judges. Maybe they'd have taken her seriously if she'd submitted something moving and dramatic instead of something campy and wacko. Who could blame the judges for tossing her DVDs right out the window? But who would give a poor, unsuspecting girl like Alexis such terrible advice?

Then there was another picture, this time of my mother. It was taken during one of her most infamous *Good As Gold* stories, a regrettable three-week period when she terrorized Shadow Canyon's pets and coeds as a werewolf. She was wearing yellow contacts and gnawing on a femur.

Underminer!

That's right, Big Bad Mama Hayden (seen here eating her young?) was leading poor Alexis around by the nose. All because she can't stand the thought of sharing the Emmy spotlight with a castmate twenty-five years younger than her. But will her scheming backfire? Some say her peers in the Academy won't look kindly on her low-down dirty scheming. If anyone's going to stop her rampage, it'll have to be them. Poor

Alexis can't do it—she cries herself to sleep at night. And not Richard Showalter, who turns a blind eye to his fiancée's tactics. Not even daughter Mallory, who for all we know is egging her on. We hear Mal's penning a hot new story for Mommie Dearest, something that will have people talking for a while to come . . . and in case you didn't guess, Sarah's nowhere near it. . . .

Whoever wrote the item definitely took a few liberties. Alexis wasn't poor, and she was about as sensitive as a sponge.

"What do you think?" Richard asked.

"Sounds dead-on to me. Although clearly, they don't know the details of the new storyline, or they would've spilled those, too."

"It's possible they'll come out later on." Richard pulled at his ever-graying hair. "You'd better hope it ends here. You think your mother's unbearable now? Just wait and see what happens if she loses out on Emmy night."

"Believe me, I'll be ready with a camera."

"In the meantime, I want to plug this leak. Whoever's talking to this Web site has inside knowledge. That narrows it down to a handful of people, including your staff of writers."

"Plus everyone at *Soap Opera Summary*. If you're going to lead a witch hunt, start there. Or on the other soap blogs. My writers don't squeal."

Whether he agreed or not, he didn't say. "As for the stuff about your mother and Alexis—"

"Anyone could have come up with that."

He looked at me curiously, like I was half bird, half bitch. "I know."

"You know her reputation. Alexis wouldn't be the first ingenue she swallowed whole."

"Just see to it you don't make any public comment until we get this sorted out."

"Anything to get me out of jumping through hoops for Kimberly. You're a doll, Richie baby."

"Don't call me that."

"Sure thing, *Dad.*" He didn't like that, either, but I didn't care. I was already out the door.

It was incredible what one piece of renegade gossip could do. Richard junked the scenes that Mom and Alexis were supposed to tape that day and sent them both home. Javier told Francesca, who told Tamika, who told me, that Mom wouldn't exit the building until security confirmed Alexis had driven off the lot. I told Tamika it was all for show. "She took a down pillow to the face, not a cement block. No way could she feel it under all the Botox."

The identity of the Likely Leaker was of less interest to the writers than the prospect of an on-set war between Alexis and my mother . . . but not for the reasons I expected.

"We're in trouble," Tamika told me. "Whether it's true about your mother or not, we can't go on with the Sarah/Vienna story. The two of them are never going to be able to work together again."

"This is a disaster," Anna said into her coffee cup.

"Months of story down the drain," sniffled Ronald.

I told them that was my problem, not theirs, and that my

first step in solving it would be to back-burner both characters . . . at least until I figured out what to do with them. As far as I was concerned, they should be rejoicing.

"No one will ever have to write Sarah preaching Wicca again. Now we can move full-steam ahead with Vienna discovering Ryan is her long-lost son."

"Woo-hoo," said Tamika. I'd seen people get more excited about oatmeal.

She wasn't the only one. That afternoon, I ran into Dallas in the parking lot.

"That was pretty crazy with your mom and Alexis today," he said.

"Were you there to see it? And if so, did you take pictures?"

"I pulled the pillow out of Alexis's hand. Not before she accidentally clocked me with it. She's got an arm."

"Here's hoping she puts it to better use at her softball game. I do not intend to lose anything more than an Emmy to *Tropical Hospital*."

"You're going?"

"Damn straight. Starting pitcher. Don't look so surprised. There's more to me than soap operas and square dancing."

"Believe me, I know. Wait a sec. Square dancing?"

"Don't tell me you've never heard of it."

"I have. I just didn't think it was what the cool kids are doing."

"You think I'm a cool kid?" I was strangely flattered. Somehow I'd thought that people stopped using the word *cool* when they hit eighteen. Maybe it just meant something else when you got out of high school. I'd have to remember to ask myself that when I graduated. "Maybe you're just out of touch," I said. "Think about it and let me know what you come up with. I have to run."

"Oh." Dallas teetered on the brink of having something to say.

"What's wrong?"

"Nothing." By which he meant the opposite. "I was talking to Richard a little while ago."

"You know that no good can ever come of that, right?"

"I'll remember that for next time. Anyway, he told me something, and I thought he was joking, but I can never tell with him. Is it true that you're going to go through with making me Vienna's son?"

I couldn't tell if he was still trying to form an opinion of the story or if he hated it but was just heroically polite.

"Nothing's set in stone."

"But it's a possibility?"

"One of several," I lied. "You don't like it."

He backpedaled. "I'm just confused. I kind of thought from our conversation at the poker game that we were going to . . ." He slowed to a stop. "Truth is . . . no, I don't like it. And you can tell I don't like it. Have you ever met an actor who can't lie?"

"No, but I guess I wouldn't really know."

"Feel free to hate me now."

Yeah, right. "I'm glad you said something. You could've just told Richard you hated it and he'd have squashed it. You didn't tell Richard, right?"

"I wouldn't do that to you. I learned my lesson the last time I interfered."

I had to reward good behavior. Not that he was a dog or anything.

"I swear we'll talk about it. Right now, I have to get to school."

"I'm sorry. Whatever you write, I'll act."

"You can't act if you have questions. And I can't write for an actor who doesn't know what he's doing. Even though my mother's performances might tell you otherwise. Let's figure this out. But I do have to get to gym. Want to take me? We can talk on the way."

He grinned at me. "Only if I get to see you square-dance."

"Sure you're cool enough?" I challenged.

Before I got into his car, I looked around to make sure nobody saw us.

Even though we weren't doing anything wrong, you could never be too sure. Not with a gossipmonger in sight.

He stared at me for a second longer before whooping, wrapping me up in his arms, and spinning me around. I may only have been inches off the floor, but it felt like forty thousand feet. It felt like flying.

f o u r t e e n

When not zipping around on his motorcycle, Dallas drove a Prius. Great for the environment, bad for me—the silent engine only amplified my inarticulateness.

"Let me see if I have this right," he said as we neared Cloverdale. "Vienna gave up her son—"

"Was *forced* to give him up," I said. "By pirates off the coast of Somalia."

"Somali pirates forced Vienna to give up her infant son, who was later sold to human traffickers, until the day he was rescued in a raid by the American navy?"

"A destroyer, specifically. The USS *Santa Barbara*."

"And the captain decided to keep the baby?"

"And name him Ryan. *Voilà*. Instant origin story."

We turned into a space in the student parking lot. Dallas didn't let go of the steering wheel. His knuckles were white.

"Or . . . maybe she just gave him up for adoption when she realized she couldn't care for a baby," I said. "I told you we had a bunch of ideas."

"And terror on the high seas was the best of them?"

Ouch. "I was joking."

Dallas relaxed his grip. "That could have come out . . . softer." He looked at me and smiled.

I wilted. It was the smile of the defeated. I'd never seen such a look on him before. It gave me the shivers.

"Aren't you under threat of expulsion or something if you don't get to gym?"

I told Dallas to forget about school for a minute. "I *had* to scrap the Ryan/Vienna affair."

"You make it sound like you didn't have a choice."

"I didn't! It had disaster written all over it. In permanent marker."

"Do you really think the audience would run screaming from their televisions if we tried it out?"

"I think Girls Aged Twelve to Seventeen would sooner take a cheese grater to their eyes than watch you lock lips with my mother."

"Is that the opinion of the head writer or of a Girl Aged Twelve to Seventeen?"

"A little of both. But it's also the opinion of a concerned party. I'm only thinking of you, you know."

"Hold up."

What did I say?

"You're junking a network-approved story, risking an Emmy, alienating your co-workers, and declaring war on your mother and Richard because of me?"

He was waiting for me to deny it. I was waiting for me to deny it. But there was no denying it.

"The one time the writers of *Good As Gold* tried to do any-thing even remotely real was when they had Geneva fall in love with her parole officer. They brought in Bill Branson, an Obie Award–winning theater actor from New York, to play the PO. For three months 'Rio and Geneva' were the darlings of daytime. They got all the covers. They got all the kudos. Until Bill's hair started falling out."

"He got sick?"

"Of my mother! And it didn't stop with Mom Pattern Baldness! Then there were migraines, followed by blurred vision and arthritis—the guy was thirty-five and a former yoga instructor!"

"Maybe he wasn't getting his vitamins?"

"Trust me, you could hook up an IV of V8 to the guy and it wouldn't straighten him out. He was just the latest in a long line of failed love interests for my mother. None last longer than a year. She's a vampire. She sucks them dry, and she'll do the same to you."

"So I'll eat garlic."

"I'm not kidding. Dallas as we know him wouldn't survive. You'd turn away from acting. You'd run screaming back to your mom and tell her she was right all along and you never should have gone into acting. You'd end up in med school."

Dallas stared straight ahead, apparently fascinated by the grove of sycamores donated by the class of '96. "You sound more like a fortune-teller than a writer."

"I'm just looking out for you."

He looked at me with those eyes of a million colors. "I wish you wouldn't. While you're looking out for me, who's looking out for you?"

"Who says I need looking out for?"

"No one, apparently." Dallas took a breath, but bit his lip, watching me and waiting. I didn't say anything. So he did. "But maybe somebody should."

I couldn't tell if he had somebody in mind, and I was afraid/curious to ask.

"It means a lot to me that you're willing to put the show on the line for my well-being," he said slowly. "But don't you know by now that I'm willing to put my career on the line for *you*? I mean, your show."

His slip—if it was a slip—was of the heel-to-banana-peel, rug-from-under-the-feet variety. It sent me flying, too. Instead of facing it, I looked at my watch.

"I'm going to be late."

The gym was my county fair nightmare come to life. Hay bales were stacked in front of the bleachers. Wagon wheels and butter churns lined the walls. Warming up on a platform was a quartet straight out of a *Hee Haw* reunion special: four overalled, knee-slapping old men, picking at banjos, fiddles, guitars, and double basses. And gingham. Lots and lots of gingham.

"Tell me there's a pie-eating contest, too," said Dallas.

"I think that would defeat the purpose of gym class. Plus there's no social engineering to be had poised over a plate of blueberry filling."

I scanned the dozens of squares until I found mine, minus me, dead center. Amelia was foaming at Keith about something, and he didn't exactly look like his serene self, either.

"Maybe you should take a seat on the sidelines," I suggested to Dallas. "Suddenly I get the feeling that your presence might not be appreciated."

How wrong I was.

"DALLAS GRANT!" shrieked Scooter, immediately shutting up Keith and Amelia. Dallas froze as the five foot seven rhino charged, to the squeals of the rest of the students. Dallas was two seconds from being flattened by Scooter's fandom—until Coach Samson stepped in to gush and took the blow himself.

Coach didn't even sway as Scooter bounced to the floor. "Huge fan, Mr. Grant—HUGE." Soon Coach was competing for Dallas's attention with the entire female and gay male Cloverdale student body. I stuck out my hand to help Scooter to his feet. Keith was there on Scooter's other side.

"Look, everybody, Dallas Grant is here," Keith muttered at me as we hoisted Scooter.

"Oh my God, I know!" said Scooter, flinging himself at the throng. He flung far short, though, crumpling and clutching his ankle.

Coach diagnosed it as a sprain ("Serves you right for not watching where you're going!") and sent for the nurse.

"Aw shucks," said Amelia with all the pretend disappointment she could muster (which wasn't much). "I guess that means we'll just have to watch. Can't square with just seven."

"No, it means you'll get an F for the day," Coach said.

"Fine by me," said Amelia as she made for the hay. "That won't even register on my GPA."

I raised my hand. "Not fine by me. An F for me is as good as not showing up. The school board will force me off the set."

"And angels wept," called Amelia, not even looking back.

Coach was sympathetic but unimaginative. "The *International Folk Dancer Handbook* is clear: Squares consist of exactly eight people. One more or less would result in an irregular quadrilateral that cannot function as a square."

"I could fill in for Scooter," offered Dallas.

The gym suddenly went quiet.

"I mean, if that's cool."

"Are you kidding?" cried Scooter, not in agony, but in ecstasy. "That's the *coolest!*"

No argument from me.

"I didn't think you were going to make it on time. Did the network revoke your chauffeur privileges?" asked Keith, loud enough to include the rest of our square in the conversation. Dallas ignored him and tried to catch up with Amelia, who wasn't having it. For some reason she was far more interested in my own domestic drama.

"We had some work issues to discuss, so he gave me a ride."

Truth or not, the look on Keith's face told me that wasn't going to cut it. I could only hope that the twang of the quartet and chicken-fried flavor of the caller's voice would help take the edge off my boyfriend.

I was doomed.

I was prepared for Cloverdale's students to rebel at the forced merriment. Or at the very least slouch. But this was LA. Put a bunch of Angelenos in cowboy costumes and give them an audience (even if it's of lower classmen), and suddenly it's everybody's next Big Break. The hoot'n'hollering started as soon as the music did. Even Amelia couldn't suppress the growing enthusiasm . . . although it probably helped that she'd traded in her partner for a bona fide hunk. Dallas threw himself into it with every ounce of his Method-actor focus, morphing from Silverlake chic to Country Lane quaint with the tap of a toe . . . only to be outshone by Keith, who stamped his foot and clapped his hands red. All this time I thought it would take a bumblebee in his boxers to spur him to dance. Turns out he just needed a little friendly competition.

"Hurry folks, fill the hall,
get your partners one and all. . . ."

And we were off. The caller warmed us up with a simple do-si-do-your-partner/allemande-left-your-corner combo—but it was quickly apparent that the dance syllabus at Juilliard favored ballet over folk. Dallas had no idea what he was doing.

And it was the most adorable thing ever.

He tripped. He stepped on feet. He turned the wrong way. He turned the right way, but too late . . . only to step on feet and then trip. He got lost in a square through, led when he should have followed, stood still when he should have led, and tried to promenade the wrong partner home (Keith). Dallas laughed an apology and even tried to dress it up, extending his hand for a shake. Keith left him hanging.

Coach popped by during a break between dances and suggested Dallas take a breather. "Probably not a bad idea," said Amelia, rubbing a bruised shin. "Maybe that way we'll avoid a trip to the ER."

"I can bow out," offered Dallas. "I don't want to cause trouble."

"Turning over a new leaf?" asked Keith.

"Hey," I said, hustling him away from Dallas. "What's wrong?"

"What's wrong is Mr. Soap Opera here sticking his nose in where it doesn't belong."

"In a high school gym?"

"In our *square*. We had a good group before Dallas barged in. You and me and Scooter and even Amelia. We were all getting along. We didn't look like idiots. And we were having fun!"

"I'm still having fun, but I guess I'm the only one not taking this so seriously."

"Maybe that's the problem. Maybe you take the wrong things seriously at the wrong times for the wrong reasons."

"Are we fighting? Because this feels like a fight. About square dancing."

"Let's just dance," Keith said, taking my hand as the fiddlers struck up another tune. Under other circumstances I would have swooned. But his touch was making my stomach turn.

I took my hand back. "Let's not. I'd rather fail than pretend everything's all kittens and puppies with you at the moment."

Amelia booed as I pivoted to walk away.

Dallas held me back. "Think: me," he whispered. "Your mom. Bedroom scene. That's what happens if you're not in the studio to steer the show."

Keith was watching. So was Amelia. So was Coach.

"Are you all going to dance or what?" Coach asked.

"Thanks for the reality check," I told Dallas, taking his hand. "Let's do this."

"What are you doing?" asked Keith.

"The acey-deucey, if I heard the call right. With my new partner. You can dance with Amelia. Maybe you'll have more fun."

"I don't know what the acey-deucey is, either," said Dallas, all smiles.

"Then I'll lead."

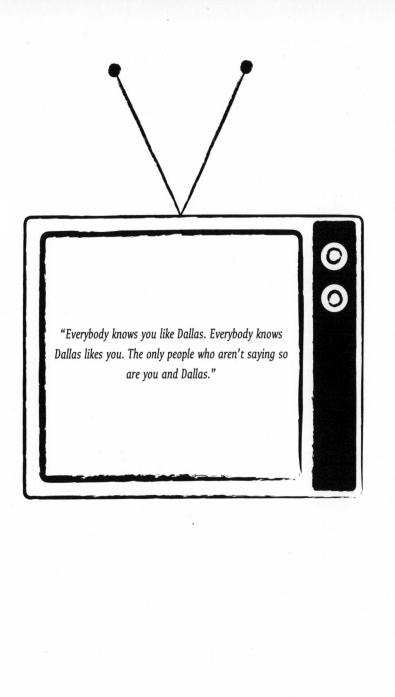

"Everybody knows you like Dallas. Everybody knows Dallas likes you. The only people who aren't saying so are you and Dallas."

f i f t e e n

malcontent: you there?
GinaBeana: Hi there, Sweetie!
malcontent: phew
GinaBeana: Are you saying I smell?
malcontent: heck no!
malcontent: never mind
malcontent: just glad you're here
GinaBeana: I'm looking up Emmy fashions!
GinaBeana: I have to look my best on the big night!
malcontent: you could go dressed in a hairnet and rubber gloves and still outshine everybody else
GinaBeana: Aw shucks, thank you. How are you?
malcontent: meh
GinaBeana: My mother used to say "meh."
malcontent: my kinda lady
GinaBeana: What's wrong?
malcontent: where to begin
malcontent: you're gonna regret asking
GinaBeana: Your disclaimer is duly noted.

malcontent: keith

rocketboy: hi

GinaBeana: What happened?

rocketboy: what's up
malcontent: working
malcontent: the usual

GinaBeana: Is it that bad?
malcontent: worse

malcontent: yourself?
rocketboy: hanging

**malcontent: all we do is
fight**
GinaBeana: What do you fight
about?

rocketboy: so

**malcontent: stuff at the
show, mostly**
**malcontent: I don't know
what to do**

rocketboy: do you want to
break up?

GinaBeana: First things first.
GinaBeana: "Stuff at the show"
doesn't cut it.
GinaBeana: You need to be
specific.
GinaBeana: And honest.
GinaBeana: Try it out.

rocketboy: do you?

GinaBeana: I know it's hard.
GinaBeana: But do your best.

malcontent: do you???

GinaBeana: Are you still there?
malcontent: yeah
malcontent: okay. my
mom, for one.

malcontent: she meddles

malcontent: she's always in
the way
malcontent: and not just
with keith
malcontent: with dallas,
too

malcontent: what?

GinaBeana: I don't think it's
your mom, Mallory.
GinaBeana: I know you two have
your problems.
GinaBeana: But she hardly even
knows Keith's name.
GinaBeana: Want to give it
another try?

malcontent: okay

rocketboy: I'm asking you

malcontent: why are you
asking?
rocketboy: because it feels like
that's what you want and I'm
not the only one who thinks so
malcontent: amelia
malcontent: right?
malcontent: that's what
you two were talking
about when I got to gym
today
rocketboy: it doesn't matter
rocketboy: I just want to know
what's up

rocketboy: hello?

malcontent: I'm here
malcontent: I feel like I
could ask you the same
thing
rocketboy: fine

169

malcontent: there's dallas
malcontent: I don't know
how to explain it
malcontent: I can't tell
what's going on
GinaBeana: Really?
malcontent: what?
GinaBeana: Mallory
GinaBeana: He likes you.
GinaBeana: A lot.
malcontent: so what do I
do about it?
GinaBeana: Depends.
GinaBeana: Do you like him?
malcontent: of course I
like him
malcontent: he's my
friend
GinaBeana: And that's all?

malcontent: well
malcontent: I mean
malcontent: I've thought
about it before
malcontent: dallas and me
malcontent: who wouldn't?
GinaBeana: No argument here.
GinaBeana: But how much do
you think about it?

rocketboy: it's dallas
rocketboy: he's into you

malcontent: that's not
true
rocketboy: oh come on
malcontent: what?
rocketboy: don't kid yourself
rocketboy: he's into you
rocketboy: way into you
malcontent: ok
malcontent: so what?
rocketboy: so are you
into him?
malcontent: I care
about him
malcontent: he's my
friend
rocketboy: that's not how it
seems to me

rocketboy: you're like a
different person around
him
rocketboy: and let's
face it
rocketboy: it's been a
while since you were
you and I was me and we
were "us"

malcontent: enough that it's a problem
GinaBeana: It is possible to fall for two people at once.
GinaBeana: That's what soaps are made of.
GinaBeana: And real life, too.
GinaBeana: Just try to keep in mind where one ends and the other begins.
GinaBeana: Unless you want to turn into Jacqueline or Sarah.
malcontent: or Vienna
GinaBeana: You could never be like Vienna.

malcontent: thanks Gina
GinaBeana: Anytime, Mal.
malcontent: night
GinaBeana: Sleep tight.
<GINABEANA SIGNED OFF AT 11:06PM>

malcontent: I know
rocketboy: so?

malcontent: I do like him

malcontent: the way you think

malcontent: but that doesn't mean I don't like you
malcontent: there was a long time when you liked me and Erika
malcontent: and you were with me and Erika at the same time
rocketboy: is that what you want?
malcontent: no
malcontent: I just want you to be patient with me

171

malcontent: the same way I had to be

malcontent: I want to try to work things out

malcontent: with you

malcontent: you

rocketboy: what about dallas?

malcontent: I have to figure that out

malcontent: I'm not sure how to deal with it

malcontent: it's so complicated

malcontent: but I don't want to break up

rocketboy: neither do I

rocketboy: I'm sorry I was a jerk today

malcontent: it's okay

malcontent: I'm sorry I was late

malcontent: I really need to get to bed

rocketboy: me too

rocketboy: talk to you tomorrow?

malcontent: sure thing

rocketboy: night, bonnie

malcontent: night, clyde

<ROCKETBOY SIGNED OFF AT 11:09PM>

malcontent: hey

malcontent: I know you're there

malcontent: I know you blocked me

malcontent: yeah, I created a second sn just to check

malcontent: yeah, it's just as you guessed, I'm that crazy

malcontent: if you don't want to respond, fine, just read

malcontent: I am going to write this just once

malcontent: I'll say it to your face, too, in case you've become illiterate

malcontent: leave keith the hell alone

chAMELIAn: bad day? go cry on dallas's shoulder

malcontent: not kidding

malcontent: blood will be spilled

chAMELIAn: you're cray

malcontent: consider yourself warned

This isn't a soap opera, *I told myself.* It's my life.

s i x t e e n

"Mallory Hayden must die," said Kimberly, unaware I'd just been conferenced in.

"Don't I know it," I said to dead silence. "So how do we do it? Poison pen seems apt."

Richard had invited me to his office for a call with the network brass. "Emmy business," he'd called it.

"Kimberly's a little on edge," announced Trip from the speaker. "You're really making her work for her money these days."

"Apparently. Has someone taken out a hit on me?"

"Marilyn Kinsey of *Soap Opera Summary*," said Kimberly. "She won't take my calls anymore. None of the soap rags will. They think we're trying to make fools out of them, giving our scoops to LikelyWhorey. And the fewer features they throw our way, the worse our chances come Emmy night."

"This is a game of chicken," I insisted. "The only reason people buy those magazines is to find out what's happening next week so they can decide whether to watch. They'll come crawling back two issues from now when the best they can manage for a cover story is 'Black Hole Eats *Tropical Hospital*.' "

"The lady's got a point. Now, enough of the bad news," said Trip. "Give them the good news, Kimberly."

"*People* is doing a piece on Mallory and Dallas."

"That'll more than make up for a dry spell at the grocery store checkout line," said Trip. There was a clink in the background, like two champagne flutes coming together.

I stared at the speakerphone, and not at Richard, lest I be tempted to smack the smirk right off his face. "Kill it," I said.

"No can do," said Trip. "They're gung ho on this story. They've already got quotes, too, from a couple of well-placed insiders."

"Like who?"

"They won't say," Kimberly told us. "They're protecting their sources."

"Offer them something else. Me and Mom, guns at dawn."

"Not sexy enough," said Kimberly. "Besides, I already tried. You know what they said about your mother when I floated it? 'We don't have an airbrush big enough to smooth out her lines.' "

"I won't cooperate. And neither will Dallas."

"Mallory," said Trip with his voice of reason, "they're moving ahead with or without you. Either you tell your side, or they tell the most gossipy story that their quotes and pictures suggest."

"So this is about my well-being all of a sudden?"

"Your well-being and that of *Likely Story* are interchangeable," said Richard.

"I seriously doubt Academy voters are going to look down

their noses at the show because Dallas and I refuse to pimp out a nonexistent relationship to the Hollywood-Industrial Complex."

"Then you're seriously overestimating the Academy," said Trip. "This is a no-brainer."

"Exactly. I'd have to be brainless and boyfriendless to pimp out a nonexistent relationship just to publicize the show. All it would do is prove to LikelyWhorey that I'm exactly the opportunist they say I am. No thanks."

"I may have to add Kimberly to my enemies list," I told Tamika in the writers' room. "You know she's one of their 'insiders.' She's probably telling *People* that Dallas and I are always meeting behind closed doors to talk about his 'motivation' or whatever."

"You have an enemies list?" she asked in disbelief.

"Only in my head."

"What else is 'only' in your head?" she mumbled from behind her laptop.

I pretended I wasn't listening. But I heard it over and over again for the rest of the day.

Richard was not above blackmail. Fortunately, he had nothing on me. But he'd already used Dallas's contract to make him jump on command. So as soon as my meeting with the writers was over, I made it my business to warn Dallas that Richard might try to rope him into the *People* interview. By the time I tracked Dallas down, he was already on the studio floor preparing to tape. I slipped into the control room and hunkered down with a copy of the shooting script. Dallas stood before my mother in Ryan's signature leather motorcycle jacket. Mom was wearing the fake tortoiseshell eyeglasses she'd insisted Vienna would wear. ("So she looks smarter?" I'd asked her at the time. "As a disguise," she said, "from the mafiosi chasing her.")

The director, a fearsome perfectionist by the name of Shelly, was about to give the go sign when she realized I'd joined them. She asked if I'd be staying to observe.

"You bet. This is a big scene."

I wasn't expecting a warm welcome. The directors resented my presence in the control room, afraid I'd take issue with their choices—which I often did. It's amazing how a director could translate JACQUELINE SIPS HER MARTINI into JACQUELINE CARTWHEELS ACROSS THE BAR DOING BODY SHOTS. Somebody had to keep them in line. Especially with the delicate material about to tape. A meth-hungry Ryan was about to tear into Vienna, neither aware that they'd later turn out to be son and mother.

Shelly pursed her lips and gave the word. The stage manager, Janet, cued the actors from the floor.

RYAN
I'm quitting school.

VIENNA
Have you already staked out
your panhandling corner?

RYAN
(HE TURNS TO GO) Think what
you want. I don't care.

VIENNA

But you hope *I* care. (RYAN
STOPS) I've never had a
dropout actually inform me of
his intentions. They just
stop coming to school.

RYAN

That would be impolite.

VIENNA

Your father raised you to
value manners. At least you
have that going for you. I
don't meet many drug-
addicted bums with good
etiquette.

RYAN

You're a guidance counselor!
You don't know anything about
me beyond my GPA.

VIENNA

I know you're scared and at
the mercy of an addiction
you're a long way from
admitting you have, much less
dealing with. That's three
things.

RYAN

                          I know a few things about
                          you, too, just by looking.
                          You drink rosé wine by the
                          boxful. Your TV is preset to
                          Lifetime on Demand. You try
                          to flirt with Mr. Vallarta in
                          the English department, but
                          part of you worries he's gay
                          and doesn't get it—or worse,
                          he's gay and *does* get it.
                     You're lonely. Washed up. And
                          you've made a career out of
                          involving yourself in the
                          lives of kids because they're
                          a captive audience. Because
                          you know deep down that no
                          man will ever invite you to
                          involve yourself in his life.
                          (RYAN STORMS OUT. *ON* VIENNA,
                                SHATTERED)

Shelly called cut and gave the order to move on to the next item. But I spoke up.

"You call that 'shattered'?"

Shelly held her tongue. I could see Mom and Dallas on the monitor, wondering whether we were going ahead or doing another take.

"Vienna's reaction in this scene sets up the next three

months of her story," I said. "What Ryan says here forces her to take a good, hard look at her life and make some changes. Right now she might as well be taking a good, hard look at her credit card bill."

"I'm not sure your mother's got another performance in her today," said Shelly. "She's a little . . . raw."

"Which is perfect for the scene. I'd be happy to give the note if it makes you uncomfortable." It was one thing for me to assert myself in the control room, but horn in on a director's relationship with an actor? Sacrilege. Shelly hupped to and marched back out onto the floor. The AD closed the boom in anticipation of obscenities . . . but strangely, no fur flew.

First Shelly gave the note. Then Mom rolled her eyes and asked a question. Shelly replied, shaping her answer with her hands, like throwing a clay pot. Mom looked at Dallas, as if Shelly were speaking Swahili. Dallas nodded at Shelly and drew Mom aside . . . and began whispering in her ear.

It was then that my mother transformed. Once an Untouchable Hardhearticon, she was now a Human Feelingbot, all shiny eyes and crinkled brow and completely alien. Dallas's smooth talking continued for a few more seconds before he turned away and resumed his place. My mother put a palm over her eyes as though the sun was beating down on her, but then I saw it: a trickle of tears escaping between her fingers. She was crying.

Shelly burst into the control room and ignored me when I asked what the hell just happened. "Roll tape and cue 'em, before she loses it!"

Mom brushed away her tears and flung her hair to one side

but otherwise did nothing to halt the scene, despite a set of vanity-killing puffy eyes. Dallas began. My jaw remained anchored to the floor for the duration of the scene.

Mom nailed it. One might even say she was Emmy-worthy.

I wound my way to Dallas's dressing room in a stupor. What had he done to tame the beast? He hadn't told her off. He hadn't questioned her ability, like Bob had all those years ago on Good As Gold. What were the magic words he'd uttered? And how much would it cost me to learn them?

I found him hunched over the sink, washing off a layer of base. "Dallas Grant: Bitch Whisperer. Who knew?"

Dallas looked up. "Oh. That. It was no big."

"No big?! I feel like I just saw Helen Keller learn to communicate. What did you say to her?"

"Trade secret. Throw me that towel?" I picked up the towel hung on the back of the door and handed it to him. "The scene turned out okay?"

"I don't think either one of you will be overlooked come nomination time next year." There was a smudge of makeup left on his temple. "You're really not going to tell me? It's a matter of national security."

"It isn't my place to say. You'll have to ask your mom." He tossed the towel on the counter and started to stuff his duffel bag.

"Then I guess I'll never know."

"Starting to regret not writing us that romance?"

I picked up the towel again. "C'mere, you're all blotchy."

Dallas stepped toward me, and I began to rub the remaining makeup from his pores.

"You do have a pretty profound effect on her," I admitted. "The only other time I saw my mom get pushed like that, somebody got fired."

"I'm not worried. She likes me."

"Runs in the family."

There was a streak of color left along his neckline. Or was that the border of a tan? Only one way to be sure. I kept rubbing.

"Say I did write that story," I suggested, noncommittal. "What happens to your fan base? All those people who love Ryan and Jacqueline?"

"Before there was Ryan and Jacqueline, there was Ryan and Sarah. People loved them, too. People love a good story and good actors. And believe it or not," he said, leaning into my touch, "your mom's the best there is on *Likely Story*."

I stopped, but didn't back off. In his presence, there was security. And certainty. He was as sure of the potential in the pairing as I was afraid of it. But he'd taken one leap of faith for me after another. I owed him.

"Okay."

Dallas started to argue, then stopped. "Did I hear that right?"

"We'll try it out. But let's keep it between the two of us until I work out the kinks. And I reserve the right to scuttle it the minute Mom lets it go to her head."

He stared at me for a second longer before whooping, wrapping me up in his arms, and spinning me around. I may have been only inches off the floor, but it felt like forty thousand feet. It felt like flying. And then I was back down, toes on the ground but still floating on air. He hadn't let go of me. I hadn't let go of him. We weren't letting go of each other. It was the edge of a kiss, and we were about to tumble over.

"You in there, Dallas?"

We sprang away from each other just as Alexis opened the door behind us.

"Bad time?" She didn't wait for an answer. "I saw your scenes on the feed just now, Dallas. Fantastic job."

Dallas turned away, but not fast enough for me to catch the white-hot look of murder he was firing at her. "Thanks."

A monosyllabic response did not appear to be hint enough for Alexis. "I wish I could get scenes like that."

"Don't look at me, I just write the show," I said with all the subtlety of a blunt instrument. Alexis left, pouting. The moment with Dallas was shot, but that wasn't necessarily a bad thing. I couldn't remember what I'd come for. All I could remember was that I had a boyfriend. But his name escaped me.

"Maybe we should talk," said Dallas.

There was no maybe about it.

"I have a story to write." I scrambled out, nearly tripping over his towel. It wasn't until I got all the way back to the writers' room that I remembered.

Keith.

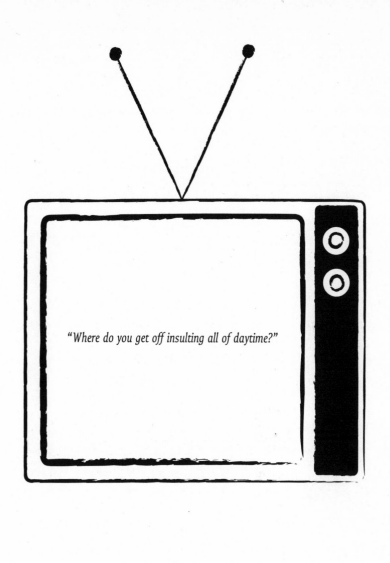

"*Where do you get off insulting all of daytime?*"

s e v e n t e e n

I went to a production meeting.

We almost kissed.

I sat in on a focus group.

We almost kissed.

I had a fitting for the Emmys.

That's what was written in my schedule.

But all I could think was: *Can they tell? Do they know? Is it written all over my face that we almost kissed?*

"What happened to you?" Mom asked when I came home.

She knows!

"What do you mean?"

"You look . . . guilty." She said it and went back to clipping her press over the kitchen counter.

"Oh." I hadn't told anyone. "Well." Not Gina, on whom I had already leaned for advice. "The thing is . . ." Not Tamika, who seemed to be souring to my personal dramas. "You're right." Not Greg. I couldn't afford for Trip to trip him up.

Mom looked back at me, thrown by the bizarre implication

that I might want to talk to her. *What am I supposed to do now?* she must have thought. *Ask her what's wrong?*

But it would take more than a nuanced performance for the camera to knock her off the top of my no-tell list. "I had some ice cream at lunch and it showed at my gown fitting."

Mom grunted, "Dairy is the Enemy," and went back to her magazines.

I wondered: If I'd waited her out, stayed silent, and forced her to respond, would she have asked me what's wrong? Dallas was of the firm belief that she wasn't all bad. Maybe I should have given her the chance to prove me wrong.

"Good job today," I blurted.

Nothing.

"You did a good job today, Mom," I said, a little louder. "Your scenes with Dallas were great."

She flipped to the end of the magazine and threw it away. "It wasn't easy, with those lines," she breathed. "But we found a way to make it work."

Her comment about the writing wasn't even a backhanded compliment. It was just backhanded. But I was undaunted.

"You and Dallas work well together."

"You're only noticing that now?"

"I'm trying to be nice."

"I taught you better than that."

"I try not to learn from your example."

"So you say."

And there we were, once again on the verge of the knock-down, drag-out brawl that capped our every run-in.

"I don't know why I try," I said, flinging my bag over my shoulder and making for my room.

"Thank you," she said, sharp enough to stop me dead in my tracks, as if the words themselves weren't enough. "Is that what you wanted to hear?"

"The only goal I ever have in mind when we talk is to not get into a pitched battle. I don't understand why you have to turn a kind word into an opportunity to tear me down."

"Oh please. You didn't tell me 'good job' because you believed it. You said it because you want me to say it back to you. You want me to tell you what an engaging script you'd handed us from on high, how lucky we are to have such a wonderful writer crafting such beautiful stories. You were fishing for a compliment of your own, Mallory. Go ahead and dump all the chum in the water you want. I won't bite."

"What would you have said if I'd told you I hated it?"

"I wouldn't have believed you then, either. Because we were as good as two sunsets seen from a Tuscan Italian veranda. Dallas's connection to me is second only to his connection to you." (This gave me pause.) "Together we're as good as gold, but you're too committed to your own agenda to conceive of it."

I could have told her right then what I'd told Dallas. But that would have been generous, and I didn't have a shred of patience to spare. "You think you know me pretty well, don't you?" I asked.

"I know you better than you know yourself. You're a pale imitation of me."

Amelia had said something to that effect once before, and I'd filled two journals debunking the idea. Now I could feel another trip to the stationery store coming on.

"Take that back!" I huffed.

"It was difficult for me to accept, too," she said, inspecting her reflection in the toaster. "But like I said, it isn't a perfect likeness. Like me, you have keen artistic senses. Unlike me, you choose to ignore them in favor of listening to your ego. You're as smart as a well-tailored tuxedo, but not smart enough to play by the rules that have kept soaps alive for seventy years."

"Soaps like *Good As Gold?*" Zing!

It barely dinged her. "Worst of all, you have talent but lack the ruthlessness to truly make the most of it."

"Meaning, I don't hurt the people I care about in order to get what I want."

"I wonder if Amelia and Kurt would disagree." *So that's what whiplash feels like,* I thought. "What do you think?"

"I think Amelia hates me, and *Keith* is pretty iffy. Maybe we're both wrong. Maybe I'm actually more you than you."

Mom waved her hand dismissively. "Let's not get crazy. You need to make a decision. Do you want Amelia and Kwame and everyone and everything associated with your life as a happy-go-lucky teenager? Or do you want to write your show? You must know by now that you can't live in both worlds. You have to choose eventually."

Richard and Tamika and Gina and Trip and probably a dozen other people had been saying that for months, ever since *Likely Story* got the green light. I still didn't believe them. With choices like those, who would?

"You'll realize it eventually," said Mom. "Maybe once the article in *People* hits, with the glut of quotes from sources at the show attesting to your flirtation with Dallas."

"How do you know about that article? Did Richard tell you?"

"Richard? Please. It was my idea."

I stopped.

"You?!"

"Don't look so appalled. They won't be writing anything that hasn't already been written on that awful Web site. They'll simply be adding some class and an air of authenticity to it."

I couldn't believe her. "How could you do this to me?"

"I'm trying to help you. You want to break up with your boyfriend, but you can't handle the dirty work. So let me be a mother and do it for you. Trust me. You and Keith will be happier in the end."

It was the first time ever she'd gotten his name right.

"You think I've gone too far," I said.
"Haven't you?"

e i g h t e e n

Keith didn't sign on to IM that night. Neither did Kevin, Karl, or Kurt. I would have called him if I didn't think the quiver in my voice would totally give me away for the *almost kisser* I was. Even though, technically, there was nothing to give away. An *almost kiss* isn't a kiss. Nobody's lips touched. No spit was swapped. A (thin) slice of air had remained between me and Dallas at all times.

Suddenly I found myself identifying with the characters on *Good As Gold* I'd always rolled my eyes at. The ones whose tiny white lies, told to protect the ones they loved, snowballed into life destroyers. Why couldn't they just tell the truth from the start?

DENIM
Thank God you survived that
avalanche.

DIAMOND
The truth is, God had nothing

197

to do with it. Ripper and I
were forced to take off our
clothes and huddle together
all night long. It was the
only way to stay warm. It
meant nothing, and I'm sure
that's the angle *People* will
take when they do their
write-up.

                    DENIM
          As in, the magazine??

                   DIAMOND
          You understand, right?

                    DENIM
        Of course. Thanks for telling
        me. Now get away from me, I
        never want to see you again.

In other words: there was no way Keith would understand.

I was allowed to skip gym the next afternoon to play in the
First Annual Alexis Randall Charity Softball Game. Mom and
Richard left a few hours early (in separate cars) for the prepara-
tory spa visit requisite for any public appearance. Richard lob-
bied hard for me to accompany them. "It'll be great blended
family bonding time," he said.

I was no fool. "Tamika's picking me up. Besides, you just want me there so she has someone else to yell at."

"How long am I in the doghouse with her? Be honest."

"Until she wins an Emmy or you convince me to give her the story she wants, whichever comes first."

"And what do I have to do to get you to—"

"Get *People* to back off."

Richard shook his head. "You know I can't do that. And I wouldn't even if I could."

"Have fun getting your roots done," I answered.

He shut up after that, and they drove off a few minutes later, leaving me alone in the house with just enough time to gather the raw material for my final assault.

Tamika nearly ran us off the 101 when I told her about my mother's latest move against me. "She's trying to break you and Keith up?!"

"She actually had the gall to say she was doing me a favor. Like I'll be a better person for having my personal life play out on supermarket checkout stands everywhere. Personally, I think she just wants to get a contact high off my publicity."

"So what are you going to do?"

"Oh good—you think I should do something. I was beginning to think you wanted me to declare a truce."

"I'm sorry I ever doubted you. Your mother is as nutty as they come, and you're allowed to defend yourself."

"I'm glad you agree."

"But I was talking about Keith and Dallas," she said. "What did Keith say when you told him what's going on?"

"He doesn't know. Eyes on the road!"

Tamika listened patiently as I explained that things between Keith and me were pretty shaky already without him learning my mother was trying to play unmatchmaker. It was bad enough that I'd told him there was something between me and Dallas, even if I didn't want to act on it. "She's probably been behind it from the start, you know," I said. "All that stuff on LikelyWhorey? The picture of Dallas and me at the end of the driveway had to be her work."

"I don't get it. What does your mother gain from messing around with your love life?"

"Who knows? Who cares? I just want it to stop. The only person who gets to make decisions about my relationships is me."

"Is there a decision to be made?" Tamika asked, receiving silence in return. "What aren't you telling me?"

I braced myself. "I like Dallas."

Tamika didn't flinch.

"And?"

"And shouldn't we be in a ten-car pileup by now? Isn't this big news?"

Tamika sighed. "Everybody knows you like Dallas. Everybody knows Dallas likes you. The only people who aren't saying so are you and Dallas."

"How do you know Dallas likes me?" Outside confirmation was invaluable.

"It's not like he confided in me over tea and scones. Let's just say it's the consensus around the studio."

"I just wish I knew what to do about it," I said as we

turned into Griffith Park beneath a canopy of slate clouds. "Keith and I are nicknames. We're the prom and road trips to Laguna. He's my boyfriend. I don't want to hurt him."

That was a trap Tamika would not be caught in. "Then don't. But just so you know, for a couple of months now, you've had the look of someone who's in exquisite anguish. Whatever you decide, try to take your own happiness into account, too." She looked at the field in front of us. "Now, take all that anguish and hurtle it into your meanest underarm pitch."

The cast and crew of *Tropical Hospital* showed up in force that day, the better to show us up. Luc (formerly Luke) Franklin, one of the *A&F Quarterly* models cast in *TH,* was already bragging to Marilyn Kinsey. "Consider this a dress rehearsal for Emmy night," he said, flexing a pec as Tamika and I passed by. (Some actors have to be bribed to take off their shirts. Others can't be paid enough to keep them on.) "We made plenty of room on our mantels for trophies."

"Bet that took you all of two seconds," I tossed over my shoulder, dragging my bat behind me like a Neanderthal's club. Marilyn and Luc were left speechless. No one ever expects a girl to trash talk.

They also never expect one to pitch. *TH*'s Teamsters assembled at the fence, scratching their heads (and other parts) as I took the mound to warm up. If only they knew . . .

My catcher bounded out to greet me and flipped up his helmet.

"Scooter?!" I gasped.

"I told Coach I had lice," he said, fluttering, "like when

Trapper faked a brain lesion to dodge the draft on *Good As Gold.* How could I miss this?! We're gonna kick some *Tropical* butt! Is your mom around?"

I told Scooter she'd probably only make it in time for the seventh-inning stretch. Then, casually, I added, "Have you seen Dallas?"

If Scooter was suspicious, he didn't show it. "He's around here somewhere. I think Alexis had him manning the pregame barbeque with Amelia."

"Say what?"

"I know, can you believe it? Alexis thought of everything. She's got all the stars dishing out hot dogs, signing autographs, playing catch with fans—do you know how many stalkers are going to show up for this softball game? I mean that in a good way."

"Go back to the part about Amelia being here," I said. "Don't tell me she's got lice, too." I thought about that for a second. "Or do," I added.

"I thought you knew. She's the one who invited me. This whole thing was her brainstorm when she started a charitable events committee for the Alexis Randall Fan Club. See?" He handed me a flyer.

Come one, come all, to the biggest Soap Opera Softball Extravagana this side of WeHo! Your favorite stars from Likely Story and Tropical Hospital will duke it out....

Scanning scanning scanning, cancer cancer cancer, batting practice, raffles, blah blah blah . . . here it was. . . .

... barbeque and more! Brought to you by the Official Alexis Randall Fan Club. Please contact President Amelia for more details!

How had I missed this? "President Amelia?! Amelia is *president* of Alexis's fan club?!" I seethed. "That makes no sense!"

"I thought it was weird, too," said Scooter. "I mean, if it was up to her, every channel would air *Judge Judy* reruns all afternoon."

I crumpled the flyer in anger, hoping too late that Scooter didn't want it for his scrapbook. "Amelia lost the lead role on *Likely Story* to Alexis. What business do they have hanging out together?"

"Well, if this was a soap opera and I was writing it, right now I'd cut to a scene with Alexis and Amelia conspiring to destroy you."

This isn't a soap opera, I told myself. *It's my life.*

When I finally caught a glimpse of Alexis, she was right where Scooter said she'd be . . . with Amelia, who happened to be standing by the grill, sliding Dallas's hot dogs into her buns.

Scooter recommended an immediate confrontation. "Break out the brass knuckles, Mal." I might have agreed with him, if there'd been a dark alley conveniently located in the middle of the diamond. But open fields are not conducive to beat downs—and besides, I told him, a big scene might have been just what they wanted. I knew it sounded paranoid. But a gossip Web site had targeted me for destruction. My mother was trying to break up me and Keith. Richard was gunning for my job. I didn't know what I was going to wear to the Emmys.

And now my two worst enemies were teaming up to fight cancer.

It couldn't get any worse.

And then the game started.

I should've known the game would go badly when my mother showed up relatively on time and Alexis invited her to kick things off with her rendition of "The Star-Spangled Banner." Alexis must have known Mom would never pass up an opportunity to perform, even though she'd unofficially given up singing five years ago, when her self-financed production of *Cats* flopped at La Jolla. Mom's Grizabella "couldn't carry a flea, much less a tune," wrote the *Times*. At least this event was only being covered by fan club newsletters.

For further distraction, there was Dallas. We did a bad job of pretending nothing was going on between us. Watercooler run-ins were fraught with drama masquerading as small talk. When I insisted he refill his bottle first, what I really meant to say was, *We almost kiss one day and you're hanging out with Amelia and Alexis the next? What's going on?* And when he still deferred to me, I'm pretty sure he was trying to say, *I'll hang out with you once you're done avoiding me.*

Amelia declined to play (her sport of choice was the Barney's Warehouse Sale Raid), instead sitting on the bleachers taking pictures for posterity. The distance she kept was of no comfort to me. I wanted her close by, the better to figure out her plan.

But my first priority was establishing my dominance over the strike zone. Mom, Dallas, and Gina covered the outfield while Tamika, Javier, Francesca, and Richard kept the infield tidy. We weren't too shabby at the plate, either. "Pretty powerful for a weasel," I whispered to Javier after Richard hit a fly deep to right. "It's all in the Wii," he responded. "He's been practicing behind closed doors in his office every chance he gets."

As the innings piled on, I began to grudgingly give Alexis and Amelia a little credit for putting the event together (though not to their faces). For the first time in forever, the entire cast and crew were all in one place, working toward a common goal. No sniping or undermining. It felt good. Like how I'd imagined working on a show would be. I didn't mind cheering Richard on, and I loved smoking Luc Franklin and all his centerfold co-stars with my fastball.

"That'll show him to clear off his mantel," I said to Tamika as we trotted back to the dugout after a three-up, three-down inning, Dallas trailing us.

"What am I missing?" he asked.

"Mallory's competitive streak," remarked Tamika. "It's been resurrected."

"Just in time for the Emmys, huh, Mal?" Dallas smiled.

Technically, the Emmys were still a few weeks away. But he was right.

Everything went south during the seventh-inning stretch. We weren't even *playing* and it nose-dived. Mom took to the field for her curtain call ("Take Me Out to the Ball Game"), and I took to the concession stand, claiming we were running dangerously low on Big League Chew. Scooter had warned me he was going to request an encore, so I took my time. Big mistake.

"Hey there," said Jake, moseying up to me. "I knew there would be payoff when I agreed to pick up Amelia."

I held up a hand, as if the international sign for stay-away-from-me-you-leprous-swine could keep him at bay. "Gmf mafay frm ee," I garbled through a mouthful of sour apple.

" 'Kiss me, Jake?' Anything you say, luscious."

He actually leaned in. So I took out my gum and pasted it on his face. "Eat it."

He was unfazed. "That's no way to treat the president's brother," he said, stretching the gum from his nose and twirling it around his finger. "You should be nicer to me. I do all of Amelia's press releases. I could start adding your name to the letterhead if you're not careful. Then you'd have no choice but to attend every single fund-raiser she ever throws."

"You know, if you put half the effort into proofreading your work that you do into torturing me, I might actually take you seriously."

"Spell-check takes too long. Besides, no one would think a fan club is for real if its newsletters went out without a few typos."

"Well, for future reference," I said, "there's a z in extravaganza."

He shrugged. "The z button on my computer sticks. You figured it out. And you're not exactly the brightest bulb, are you? Shapely . . . just not bright."

I felt like I could pick up a disease just talking to him.

"Is there a problem here?"

Jake and I turned to see Dallas.

"Everybody's climbing the walls waiting for the gum, Mallory," he said.

"We're kind of having a conversation here," said Jake.

"It looks pretty one-sided to me," said Dallas.

I agreed, and took Dallas's arm to lead him away before things got any tenser.

"But, Mallory," cried Jake, "you forgot your gum!" I didn't have to look behind me to know it was wadded up and displayed on the end of a certain finger.

Dallas and I walked back to the field, silent most of the way.

"Does that guy skeeve you out as much as he skeeves me out?" he asked.

"Nah . . . Jake's a walking health-code violation, but ultimately he's pretty harmless." I was keeping mum, mostly because I didn't know how to broach the subject of our encounter the other day. It would have been so much easier, at least in the short run, if we didn't mention it. But it had to be done. I just wished it didn't have to happen while I was wearing tube socks and Umbros.

"We kind of had a moment, didn't we?" I asked.

"I feel like we've had a bunch of moments. That one in my dressing room was just the biggest and latest one," Dallas said.

"Maybe you're right," I admitted.

"I should've told Alexis to beat it right away." He sighed.

"And I shouldn't have run out. I got kind of overwhelmed. A lot of things hit me all of a sudden."

"Keith," he said.

"Definitely Keith."

"No," said Dallas, pointing. "Keith."

I looked toward the dugout and saw Keith in his CPK

uniform balancing a stack of pizza boxes as Alexis pushed a bundle of cash into his pocket.

"Maybe now isn't such a great time to talk," Dallas said.

"No kidding." I watched as Keith followed Alexis to a table and saw Dallas and me in the process.

It looked like Alexis and Amelia had thought of everything.

Keith had ditched work to watch the rest of the game. Under other circumstances, I might've appreciated the support, but he didn't do a lot of cheering. Mostly he sat in the stands and stared at Dallas, like a sniper waiting for the "go" signal. My distraction did wonders for *TH*'s batters. Dallas and Gina spent the top of the eighth and top of the ninth chasing down runaway fly balls (Mom was of no use with her lazy lope).

By the time Luc Franklin took the plate in the ninth inning, I was drained. I could no longer bring the heat, and my curveball had all the swerve of a training bra. Three pitches in quick succession were way out of the strike zone, and I was in danger of loading the bases. That's when Alexis—my manager—emerged from the dugout and made her way to the mound. The infield brought it in.

"I think we've come to the end of the road," said Alexis unapologetically.

"Now, hold on a second," said Francesca. "Mallory held them scoreless for eight innings."

"But her mind has mysteriously gone elsewhere, taking her pitching arm with it. She can't close it out," said Alexis, "and we need a win."

"What for? There's no World Series of Soap Softball," I said.

"Exactly," said Tamika. "We're playing for the kids."

Richard was getting impatient. "But the kids have already won. They're getting their cancer cure. We're playing for bragging rights. Do any of you want to lose to these jokers? A bunch of over-tan, over-hyped, over-emoters? Do any of you want to send Luc Franklin and his posse of *brahs* on their way with a trophy they can lord over us on the red carpet in a few weeks' time? Or do you want to walk out of here winners?"

"Thank you, Coach," I said. "Look, I don't want to lose any more than you do, but it doesn't look like Alexis planned for this contingency. Or do you have an all-star in your back pocket?"

Javier actually looked at Richard's back pocket.

"Just let me finish this," I continued. "I promise we'll go out with a bang."

Richard opened his mouth to protest.

"And we'll get a ton of press out of it."

He shut his mouth.

"Just do me one thing: Be ready."

Tamika didn't like the tone of my voice. "For what?"

"You'll know."

They headed back to their positions. Scooter hung back. "Do you really have a couple of strikes left in you, Ace?"

"Probably not. I refuse to lose this game, Scooter. But I don't think I'm going to be able to win it, either. At least not the old-fashioned way."

"I don't think there are ties in softball, Mallory."

"No. But there are forfeits. You have health insurance, right?"

I told him my plan, and he returned to the backstop, crouching down behind Luc, who took a few practice swings and stepped up to the plate. Scooter looked at me and signaled between his legs. Two fingers. I nodded and began my windup, just as Scooter said something under his breath to Luc. Before I released the ball, I saw Luc flinch and dart a glance at Scooter.

"STRIKE ONE!"

Scooter tossed the ball back to me. Luc replied to Scooter, forcefully enough to send a few flecks of saliva twirling from his lips. Whatever he said, it was blue enough to shock the ump, who did a double take. Scooter, unperturbed, got back into position and signaled: three fingers. I took my sweet time getting ready for the next pitch, allowing Scooter an eternity to up the ante. He mouthed off to Luc once more, and the strain on Luc was clear even from my perch on the mound. Despite the slothlike speed of my pitch, Luc caught nothing but air.

"STRIKE TWO!"

Luc now turned and faced Scooter full on. Scooter showed his hands, as if to say, *I'm unarmed.* The ump got between them. People in the stands sat up and took notice. The *TH* dugout bristled, and I made sure to make eye contact with all the people on my team, sending them my telepathic message: *This is it. I hope.*

The ump succeeded in separating Scooter and Luc, which was not the easiest thing to do, given the height and weight and muscular advantage Luc had. Luc prepped himself in the batter's box, trying to shake off Scooter's mysterious insults. I looked to Scooter for his signal: five fingers. He was about to go all out. I made a promise to myself, and to God: *If this works, I will write into* Likely Story *one plot of Scooter's choosing, even if it involves trapping Ryan in a genie's bottle.*

I gripped the ball, reached back, threw—and caught Luc looking.

"STRIKE THREE!"

"No way!" screamed Luc. *Now* I could hear what he was saying. "This is bull!" He slammed his bat to the ground and got in the ump's face. First came the obscenities. Then came the gesturing. Then came the dirt kicking. Then came the ump, throwing Luc out of the game. Then came Scooter with the coup de grâce: one last barb, the only words of which I caught were *momma* and *wuss.*

And then came Luc, charging poor Scooter. Then came me, Tamika, Richard, Javier, and Francesca charging Luc. Then came the emptying of the *TH* dugout onto the field and into the fray. Then came Gina, Dallas, Keith, and even Mom, pulling and pushing and, yes, even hitting (or in some cases, slapping). Then came the fans. Then came the cops. Then came the black eyes and fat lips. Then came the reporters. And then came the lawyers. Then came the publicity.

And then, finally, came Richard's smile.

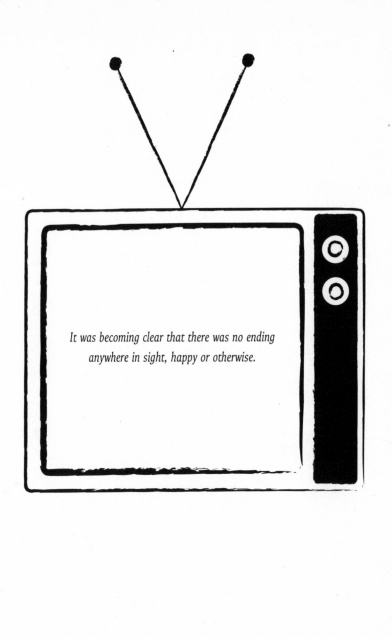

It was becoming clear that there was no ending anywhere in sight, happy or otherwise.

n i n e t e e n

The comments Scooter made to inflame Luc were the subject of much speculation, from Cloverdale's gym locker room (where Scooter gained new celebrity status) to the studio's makeup room. Luc wasn't talking, and the ump didn't squeal, either. (Richard maintained that Luc bought his silence.) Scooter was keeping mum, too, but for dramatic purposes. "Make 'em laugh, make 'em cry, make 'em *wait*" was what he said whenever I begged him to dish the dirt. Word of Scooter's philosophy got back to Trip, who briefly considered hiring him as a consultant, until Richard applied the brakes, saying that he already had enough teenagers to deal with.

Spirits were high at the studio in the wake of the softball brawl. The network even sent another gift basket: dried fruit. It was unclear whether this was a step up or a step down. The lumps we took on the field were war wounds, proudly displayed. "See this?" asked Javier, rolling up a sleeve for a trio of burly electricians. "Teeth marks. *Tropical Hospital*'s third baseman and resident amnesiac bit me!" They were duly impressed.

"And when it was all over, he asked me out! I hope he doesn't forget my number!"

There was no way I was messing with this success, not even to clarify my situation with Dallas. *Nothing happened,* I was back to reminding myself, and the farther away from him I stayed, the surer I could be that it would remain that way.

I even began to seriously consider the unthinkable: dropping my vendetta against my mother. The end of the Emmy voting period was fast approaching, and the ceremony was right after it. I still had in my possession the silver bullet that could cripple her dream, but if I was going to take aim and fire, I had little time left to do it.

Maybe I won't have to, I thought. *Maybe I blew this all out of proportion.*

But my mother couldn't leave well enough alone.

Keith needed a tux for the Emmys, and I needed to be there when he picked it out. I'd offered to hook him up, but he adamantly refused my charity, especially when he already had something (his words) "totally right" for the occasion: a powder-blue number, a family heirloom that he once wore ironically to a future-themed sophomore dance. I didn't "hate" the idea, but ran it by Gina as she gave Richard a trim and Alexis waited for her daily flatironing. Gina was totally in favor of anything "different." But Richard nixed it and Alexis backed him up. "Do you *want* the people from *E!* to make a fool out of your boyfriend on national TV?" she squealed. She had a point. I'd already made a fool out of him on the Internet and in print. One more strike and I'd be out.

"Here's what you do," said Gina. "I know a guy who runs a tux shop at the Beverly Center; we used to send a lot of business his way whenever *Good As Gold* shot a wedding, which for a three-year period in the late eighties was once every six weeks. Take Keith there this afternoon and drop my name. That way you're not paying for it and neither is he. Keith will be rolling in comped Armani by sundown."

Later, Keith rolled up to the studio in his Mustang and we headed for the mall. He clung to my hand between shifts.

"Sure you can handle this baby and me at the same time?" I asked. "Wouldn't want you to dent a fender."

"What's a little chrome between lovers?" He dropped that last word like he was test-driving it. He was definitely interested, but not yet ready to make a down payment.

I got caught looking.

"What? Is my hair messed up?" he said.

"Lovers?" I teased.

"Is that weird?" he asked.

"Not if we're disillusioned Cold War spies, faking our deaths to run off together to Fiji."

"All you had to do was say it's weird," he grumbled. He glanced in his rearview mirror and waved at the driver tailgating us. "Go around if you don't like my driving. . . ."

"It's cute," I insisted. But *cute* won me no points. I should've known. Few guys are enlightened enough to take it as a compliment. "But whatever happened to girlfriend/ boyfriend?"

"That's what *I* said," Keith busted out. "But your friend the reporter was all, 'That sounds so *high school*.' So I said, 'Uh, sweethearts?' No, too old folks home. 'Steady?' Too preppy. 'Boy toy/ladylove?' Too sarcastic. It went on like that until I told her that I only had twenty minutes left before Universal Themes class, so she'd better move the interview along."

Alarms were going off in my head. "Okay, hold on," I said. "Reporter friend? *Interview?*"

"And that's another thing! When exactly were you going to tell me about that?" Keith griped. "I could've used a heads-up. Especially when she started asking about you and Dallas."

That sudden gnawing in the pit of my stomach was the feeling of my soul trying to dig itself a place to hide from Keith's sidelong stare.

"What did she want to know?" I asked slowly.

Keith was darting glances to and from his rearview mirror.

"Just pass me already!" he complained.

"Why would she ask you about me and Dallas?" Like I didn't already know the answer. I just wanted to see if Keith did, too.

"I dunno, maybe somebody besides me and Amelia and all those bloodhounds on the Internet finally figured out that you and Dallas look a little more like you and me than you and me do. All I know is, I spent my whole study hall trying to convince this woman that you and Dallas are just friends and that you and I are still together. And now all I can think of are what kinds of verbs and adjectives she's going to use to describe me in *People* freakin' magazine. Struggling? Lackluster? Clueless?"

"You're none of those things," I promised him. "And I'm sorry you got blindsided. I was hoping I could stop it from getting this far."

"Stop what?" he asked, coming dangerously close to anger. "The article? Or the reason it's being written?"

Both, actually. But I didn't know how to tell him that. I didn't know how to tell him that my mother thought he was holding me back. That she thought we should break up. That she was actually trying to make that happen. That from her cracked point of view, she was doing for me what I couldn't do for myself. And that she might be right. That the more distance I kept between Dallas and me, the closer we got. That I'd asked Keith to give me time to smother my feelings for Dallas, but I'd wound up fanning the flames instead. That despite the desperate guarantees I'd made myself that *nothing happened*, something most definitely would have if not for Alexis's timely arrival. And that something kept trying to happen.

The bottom line was, I didn't know how to hurt him.

But looking at him now was almost like looking at a stranger. His fingernails were chewed to the pink. His once serene surfer's face was now always carved with one worry line or another.

I'd thought I didn't know how to hurt him . . . but the truth was, I'd become an expert at it a while ago.

I took a deep breath. *Keep it simple,* I told myself.

"My mother set up the *People* interview behind my back. She's trying to break us up."

Keith flung a look at me. "Seriously?"

"Keith, watch out!" I shrieked.

Keith slammed the brakes, and we came to a flying halt one foot short of the Benz in front of us. "Are—are you okay?" he stammered.

But just as I caught my breath, it was knocked out of me again as the car jolted forward, bumped from behind. We froze for a moment, his hand on mine as we both awaited the aftershock of a chain reaction crash, but none came. I guess the other drivers knew better than to drop bombs while cruising the highway.

"I'm fine." I was trembling when Keith checked in again. "Are you okay?"

Keith nodded, but the sickly color of his face told otherwise. "I'm afraid to look at the car," he said.

"Do you want me to?"

Keith shook his head forlornly, like I'd offered to identify the body of a presumed-dead loved one. "No. I should be the one." He unbuckled his seat belt and opened the door, right into the bright pop of a flashbulb.

"What the hell?"

The paparazzo who'd rear-ended us snapped away. "Why'd you stop short, Keith? Are you drunk? Are you high?"

"Did you follow us out of the studio lot?!" I yelled.

Keith shoved past the paparazzo and crept to the back of the Mustang, terrified at what he might find. I craned my neck and looked out the back windshield. The blood returned to Keith's face . . . with the force of a tidal wave. The paparazzo was oblivious to the transformation Keith was undergoing, from mild-mannered SoCal high school student to 150-pound Hulk in All Stars and J.Crew.

"Were you and Mallory in a fight? Is it about Dallas? Has he finally come between you?"

Keith dived at the paparazzo, and the two fell to the

pavement, wrestling for control of the camera as I heard the faint siren of an approaching police cruiser.

By the time it was all said and done, news copters buzzed overhead, Keith was handcuffed, the camera was broken, and so was the paparazzo's pinkie. We'd made the local news and then some.

In other words, my mother had gotten her way yet again.

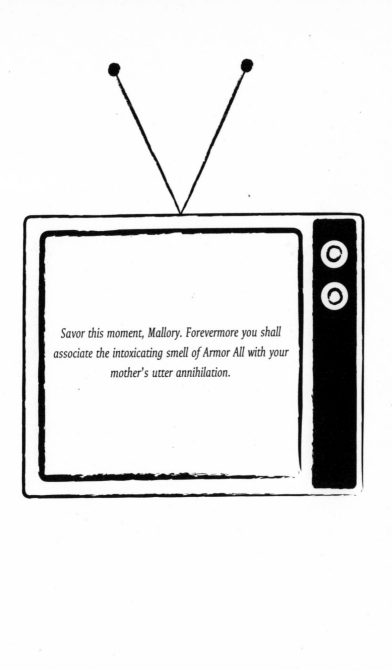

twenty

After bailing Keith out, and trying to defuse his understand-
able rage, I headed for my computer, hoping I could get back
into my writing world and shrug everything off. But I couldn't.
There was no way. My characters seemed fake to me—I had to
deal with the real people in my life first. I was angry, and anger
makes you do stupid things. Like create a new e-mail address
called SetSideSource. And use it to shoot off a message to
www.likelywhorey.com. I should have been yelling at the mysterious person who ran the site, blaming him or her for ruining
my life. But really, he or she was just a mosquito in my ear,
compared to my mother, who was a tapeworm in my gut. And
that tapeworm had to be destroyed. I went to her safe, the one
hidden behind her Roy Lichtenstein painting. My mother
could memorize ninety pages of script, no problem, but when
it came to numbers, she became a goldfish. So all of her com-
binations were the same—our home phone number. I got the
document I needed, scanned it in, replaced it, then added the
scan as an attachment to my e-mail. Did I hesitate a second
before hitting send? Yes—but only a second.

This was, after all, war.

Not twenty minutes later, a post was splattered across the LikelyWhorey site.

Old As Gold!

BREAKING! According to a copy of the diva's birth certificate (SEE below) just now forwarded to us by a trusty anonymous informant, the veteran star of Good As Gold and Likely Story could be eligible for the senior discount at The Ivy. It's widely known that she's long claimed to be forty years old, but by our calculations, she actually weighs in at a whopping **SIXTY! HOW** on earth did no one know this?! **WHY** isn't this sexy sexagenarian owning up to her age?! WILL this shameless lie blow her chances for an Emmy?! And perhaps most importantly, enquiring minds need to know: Just **WHO** is your plastic surgeon, Ms. Hayden?! DEVELOPING . . .

Someone from the network must have been monitoring the site at all hours, because it wasn't ten minutes before Mom's phone rang. I wasn't close enough to hear her answer. But when she found out, her bloodcurdling screams filled the house.

They would ring in my ears for hours.

Maybe someone, somewhere would think I looked like a winner.

twenty-one

When news of Mom's sudden-onset Soap Opera Rapid Aging Syndrome hit the public, she hit the wall and everything else hit the fan.

It was practically still dark the next morning when the network's publicity heads darkened our door. Mom's rivals hadn't wasted time. Georgina Devereaux, Anastasia Driscoll, and Westerly Easton had all gotten together and drafted a press release saying that the "fabrication about her age constitutes a fraud against the Academy's electorate, who cannot be expected to make an informed choice without such vital information."

"Those jealous harpies. They're just afraid of losing to their better," she swore, more to herself than to anyone else.

"Anastasia's had it out for you ever since you faced off on *Celebrity Family Feud*, remember?" soothed Richard. "When you made mincemeat out of her during the Name Something Oprah Winfrey Can't Live Without category."

"Survey says . . . Gayle King," said Mom, smiling softly.

"And then there's your looks," Network Publicist #1 chimed in. "We intend to let your face do most of the talking."

"The best thing would be if we could prove the Web site's copy of your birth certificate is a forgery," mused Network Publicist #3.

"Well, that shouldn't be too difficult," said Richard, turning to Mom. "Don't you have a copy?"

Mom stood staring out the bay window, apparently deaf.

"Hon?"

Mom didn't move. "I do have one," she murmured. "In the safe. Behind the Lichtenstein. I checked. It's still there."

"Of course it's still there, darling. It isn't as if someone broke in and stole it."

Now seemed to be a good time to excuse myself.

"And it's not like anybody's going to walk out of the Hall of Records with the original, right?"

For a moment Mom said nothing, just leveled her thousand-yard stare out past the swan pond.

"Of course not. You don't really think I'd be stupid enough to leave evidence like that lying around, do you?"

Richard and the publicists froze. "Do you mean to say . . . ?" Richard began.

"You might as well know," she said. "The truth seems bound and determined to come out, anyway. I'm just the age they say I am."

Publicist #2 coughed.

"Does anyone have a cigarette?" asked Mom.

The publicists didn't hang around much longer. Their entire angle hinged on my mother actually being the forty-year-old she'd claimed to be. Now it was back to square one. Not long after that came the second blow of the day: Richard bailed. I hunkered down behind the banister, the best spot in the house from which to watch my mother's relationships eat themselves alive.

"What else are you hiding?!" Richard screamed, scraping a layer of vocal chord from his throat in the process. "Nazi gold?"

"I don't see what the big deal is," she stammered to the tune of pouring vodka. "This is Hollywood. We're Daytime. Everyone lies about their age."

"By twenty years??"

"I have my reasons, none of which I need to explain to you. If you were so curious to know how old I am, all you had to do was ask."

"Let's imagine that conversation, shall we?" he offered. "Me: Exactly how old are you? You: Old enough. Me: No, really. You: Sixty. Me: No, really. You: No dialogue, you just pick up a knife and gut me."

"If it's a crime to look marvelous, then I'm guilty as charged! But since when has it been against the law to market oneself as one pleases? People will believe what they want to believe. I refuse to stand here and be judged for not getting in their way . . . and certainly not by a man with *your* past." I had no idea what that meant, but I made a mental note to look into it later.

Richard was quick to correct her. "I've been up-front about my past from the start. This is something else altogether. I don't know how we come back from this."

"You mean you don't know how *you* come back from this,

don't you? That's what you're worried about. You're afraid no one will take you seriously now."

Richard leaned in close. "Do you think I'd have proposed to you in the first place if I was at all concerned about my reputation?"

I noticed that the concept of love seemed to bear no relevance to the subject at hand.

Mom leaned in closer still. "I've seen your Internet search history, Richard. I know you Google yourself every morning."

"You would, too, if you were me. Before our engagement, I could look myself up and the first ten links would be about my credits. But now I have to sift through pages of 'cougar bait' Web sites just to find a mention of my ACE Award!"

"Believe me," Mom responded in a low tone, "there are worse things in life than being thought of as sexy."

"Well, if you're waiting for thanks, forget about it. You've got a better shot at winning an Emmy."

Mom actually recoiled.

"I want you out of here," she demanded.

She'd tolerated his childishness, low blows, and self-centeredness with ease, mostly. But implying she'd come up empty at the Emmys was grounds for eviction. Richard was rattled.

"Good," he lied. "I don't want to be here."

She saw him to the door. I scooched back a few feet, just out of sight. Even so, I heard his parting shot all too clearly.

"I've done nothing but prop you up from day one," he said. "With Trip, with Alexis, with Mallory. Good luck finding someone else to be your human crutch." Then he was gone, disappearing behind a slammed door.

She waited a moment. And then she started to cry. Real tears. And I sat on the stairs, paralyzed.

All I'd wanted to do was teach my mom a lesson. Maybe put the fear of Mal into her. And if she lost out at the Emmys again, so be it. Wrecking her engagement to my boss was not what I'd bargained for. At least not today.

The studio could not shut up about the Hayden family dramas. From the moment I walked in Monday morning, it was one question after another. "Does your mother still have both her hips?" "Is she taking her calcium?" "Does she drink the blood of unicorns?"

Yes.

As far as I know.

It wouldn't surprise me.

Tamika's was the one question I didn't have an answer ready for.

"Are you happy now?"

Ronald and Anna were already waiting for us in the writers' room, so I dragged Tamika into the office supply closet and closed the door behind us.

She went on. "Because you don't look it. You ought to be doing a jig. A bright, holy light ought to be shooting out of your bottom. Didn't you finally get what you wanted?"

"Hard to say," I replied. "Why? What have you heard?"

"Just that your mother's alienated the Academy. And that Richard's sleeping in his office tonight, because the Mondrian's booked solid. And that Keith has a court date for decking some paparazzo."

"That's basically what I know."

"Then you hit the trifecta," she said, arms crossed. "No way is your mom going to win now. Richard's probably going to dump her. And you can dump Keith with clean hands. I mean, who wants a boyfriend with a record?" From anyone else, that last question might have been rhetorical. But Tamika wanted to hear what I had to say.

"You think I'd dump Keith just because he got arrested? Again?"

"I don't know what you'd do or not do anymore." She sighed. "I used to think trying to sneak a few sex jokes past the network censors was your limit. Now I'm beginning to think I was way off base."

This was the kind of comment that begged for follow-up. She'd probably spent a couple of hours crafting it. Tinkered with it some. Subbed a metaphor here, pared it down there. It was designed to elicit a response, and from that response a decision—maybe a really momentous decision—would be made about the future of our friendship. The same thing had happened more than once with Amelia as our friendship was circling the drain, only I was too chicken to admit it at the time. I might have been able to salvage things if I hadn't made promises I couldn't keep, and if I'd told her the truth about her chances of getting cast from the very start. But every time one of those moments arose, I shied away from confronting it head-on, instead preferring to delude myself that something neat and clean was bound to happen, some way out would avail itself, something that would give everybody the happy ending they wanted.

It was becoming clear that there was no ending anywhere in sight, happy or otherwise.

"You think I've gone too far," I said.

"Haven't you?"

"What else was I supposed to do, roll over and let Mom and Richard run me into the ground? If I'd played ball with them, Vienna would be *Likely Story*'s main character, Richard would have the power to ground me, and I'd be going to the Emmys alone! Why should I have to apologize for defending myself?"

"You shouldn't," Tamika sniffed. "But all you needed to do was disarm them. Instead, you ripped their arms off. The two people who are arguably your biggest fans. Like it or not, *Likely Story* wouldn't have been made without them. Now you're in a position to return the favor and help make your mom's dream come true. She's nominated for an Emmy. The thing she wants most in life. But instead of getting out there and stumping for her, you do everything you can to ruin her chances."

"But can't you see—it shouldn't be the thing she wants most in life!"

Tamika sighed. "I know, I know. Still—why take it so far?"

"How else was I going to get my point across?" I pleaded.

"Have you really gotten it across? The only way for them to know not to mess with you is for them to know *you're* the one messing with *them*! So when exactly are you going to take credit for airing your mom's dirty laundry on the Internet?"

I hadn't thought of that. Somehow I just figured they'd know instinctively that I was the evil mastermind.

"I thought so," Tamika said sadly before brushing past me to walk out.

"Wait a second, where are you going? I need your help to figure this out. I can't talk to anyone else about this!"

"Exactly. I'm hardly your friend anymore, am I? I'm your talk-to. I get the brunt of all your crazy scheming because you can't unload on anyone else. Which means there's no time in our conversations for anyone but you. Do you even know that I'm going stag to the Emmys? Or that I moved to Santa Monica?"

All I could do in response was stare at her dumbly.

"I didn't think so. If you need advice on how to deal with your mother and Richard, you're going to have to look elsewhere. That subject is officially off-limits. It's the only way this thing we call our friendship will survive."

A few hours later, I took a break, leaving Ronald, Anna, and Tamika to wrestle with the network's latest challenge, an "opportunity" to situate bathroom cleanser in a teenage milieu. I wasn't in a product placement kind of mood. The head honchos suggested we feature the soap scum remover by having Ryan get a job as a nude maid. I suggested instead that Jacqueline could use it to spike Sarah's shampoo.

It was more Tamika's idea than mine that I take a break. "Vengeance is not conducive to storytelling," she told me.

So I wandered the studio looking for a friendly face, but was met with mistrust everywhere I went. Department heads scattered as I drifted near, obviously true believers of Richard's tales that I was a teenage micromanager, a rare and fearsome beast of the Hollywood veldt. He'd spread that rumor early on, just as the shared euphoria of the show's first episodes began to wear off. I wasn't savvy enough at the time to understand the rumor's meaning and undo the damage. So everyone shunned me and looked to him. If there was ever a guy who knew how to consolidate power, it was Richard.

This wasn't the way I'd remembered it being on *Good As Gold*. I'd had the run of the studio when I was little. Gina would send me on errands that took me all over the building, and sometimes the lot. In the process, I got to know everyone, and they got to know me. I wound cord for the electricians (and was given honorary union membership) and forged autographed head shots for the drunker actors, and no one treated me like I was a kid. I was part of the team. But now I wondered if I'd been wrong from the start. Maybe there'd never been a "team" in the first place. Maybe I'd just been too young to see it. Maybe nobody did things for the good of the show. Maybe they just did things for the good of themselves. Maybe I'd become one of those people.

And then, standing in the middle of the studio floor, deserted for the lunch break, I saw it.

Sitting in Ryan's bedroom set, at the foot of the bed.

The trunk.

I'd last seen it in Geneva's mayoral office on *Good As Gold*. I knew our set designer had swiped some furniture pieces from Mom's old show when it was going under, but I had no idea that my favorite hiding place had been saved from a life sentence in the back of a prop house.

I kneeled in front of the trunk, hooked my fingers under the lid, and lifted it open, its familiar creak music to my ears. The My Little Pony stickers with which I'd decorated the interior were still there, plastered to the inside until the end of time.

I climbed in. Incredibly, I still fit, although it was much

more cramped than it used to be. I let the lid close on top of me and inhaled the dark and musty scent. *Move over, New Car Smell; Old Trunk has got you beat, hands down.*

I closed my eyes and a trunkful of memories hit me. Flashlights and spiral-bound notebooks. Scribbled plans and diary entries. The things I'd heard from within: whispered secrets, stilted performances, bad dialogue, thrown punches, torn clothes, cries of passion, cries of torment, cries of mercy, cries of joy . . .

I could have stayed like that, lost in the past, for hours. I drifted off into that blurry zone between sleeping and remembering. Then two muffled voices brought me back.

"I heard she threatened to quit," said Voice #1.

"I heard she threatened to have Richard fired," said Voice #2.

The first thing I thought was: *There are two people sitting on your trunk.*

"Come on. Not even she can pull something like that. There are limits to her powers," said Voice #1.

"You just don't have any imagination," declared Voice #2.

The second thing I thought was: *You know these voices.*

#2: "Here's what I call power. . . . She single-handedly shot to hell Alexis's chance at getting an Emmy nomination. You do know that, right?"

#1 blew a raspberry. "Soap legend and sour grapes. Don't believe what you read on the Internet."

The third thing I thought: *I should join this conversation.*

#2 was positive: "Everything that's happening to Old Lady Hayden now is chickens coming home to roost. Karma's a bitch."

#1: "She's totally going to hunt down whoever leaked her birth certificate to those LikelyWhorey lunatics."

#2: "Woe betide those who cross an aging soap star. Or her daughter."

Fourth thought: *Don't do anything hasty, Mallory.*

#1, after a silence: "What's that supposed to mean?"

I imagined #2 shrugging all innocent-like: "I wouldn't want to mess with Mallory. Would you?"

#1: "I already have, and I lived to tell the tale."

#2 snorted: "Mallory Hayden would spare you if you set a puppy mill on fire."

#1: "Don't go there, Francesca."

Fifth: *The identity of #2 has been confirmed.* And given that there was just one person in the entire studio with whom Francesca thought she could be herself with, that meant #1 was almost certainly . . .

Francesca: "Whatever you say, Dallas."

"I hope she's okay."

"She'll turn up."

"Greg says she's been missing for hours. She left her cell phone and her bag in the office."

"Which means she's coming back," Francesca insisted. "She's probably just hiding out somewhere, dreaming up new stories to tell or ways to torture her mother. Why aren't you out looking for her, if you're so worried?"

"Because if she knew I was trying to find her, she'd probably just run farther away. Ever since our square dance, she can hardly stand to be in the same room with me. If I'd known my do-si-dos were that bad, I'd never have set foot in that gym."

"I don't think it's your dance moves, or lack thereof, that are putting the distance between you two." Francesca chuckled.

"What's that supposed to mean?"

"You told me not to go there." She sighed. "So I won't. Just try not to worry so much about Mallory, okay? Look at this place. If it wasn't for her, there would be a studio audience on this set watching the network's answer to *The View*. Everybody here has a job because of her. You and I are members of SAG because of her. You have an Emmy nomination because of her. People have mortgages because of her. She's taking care of herself and everybody else at this show. She knows what she's doing."

It was nice to hear someone else say that, especially because it wasn't said to my face. The fact that it was anything but true was an afterthought.

"I know she does," said Dallas. "I just wish she knew that she doesn't have to do it alone."

I'd finally found what I was looking for. I just couldn't face him.

Not yet.

Sixteen years of growing up in LA and watching my mother manipulate the media had trained me for this moment.

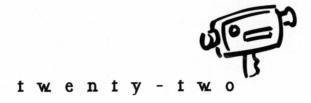

t w e n t y - t w o

Dallas seemed to think I was drowning, but I was intent on proving him wrong. Even if it meant swimming with my Great White Mother.

Nobody knew how the Twenty-Year Gap would affect Mom's chances. Some women (and more than a few gay men) were rallying behind her, saying sixty was the new forty, anyway.

As the day got closer, Mom started eating less and less. Not out of a desire to fit into her dress, but out of sheer nervousness.

If it had been bad before, when she hadn't been nominated at all, now it was even worse. Because now it was about having a shot—and losing anyway.

I really didn't think about my own chances.

Like everything else, this was all about my mother.

The big day arrived, and there was no way for me to stop it. I got into my Calvin Klein sea foam sheath dress and was ready to take a look at the whole product, finally put together. I hesitated before facing the mirror. Dressing up these days often left me cold. It hadn't always been that way. There was a time I'd loved exploring my mom's closet, especially sifting through the section reserved for "never agains." These were items she kept on hand to remind herself of the bad old days, when sequins and shoulder pads ruled. "Those who forget history are doomed to repeat it," she'd say, shuddering. I'd mix and match the plaidest blazer I could find with a polka-dot skirt, then pose for the mirror, reciting *Good As Gold* dialogue by heart. Once, Mom caught me doing one of her juicier speeches.

"*I* own Shadow Canyon Hospital now," I proclaimed in my best Geneva voice. "And that means I get to pull the plug on anyone I want. So sayonara, Mr. Secretary-General!"

Mom was not impressed.

"More attitude," she directed impatiently. "Geneva thinks the United Nations is a joke."

I tried, but Mom had a knack for arrogance that I'd yet to match.

"We can't all be performers, can we?" she said, relieved. "I'm sure there are other things you can do with your life."

I was seven.

I'd since discovered that she was right—there *were* other things I could do with my life . . . things that could get me Emmy-nominated. I didn't need pretend reasons to get dressed up. I had perfectly legitimate ones. Pep talk concluded, I stepped in front of the mirror and was not displeased with what I saw. Maybe someone, somewhere would think I looked like a winner.

"Greetings from 1979," said Keith when he arrived not long after. He was wearing his father's powder-blue tux. Between school and work and court dates, we'd never gotten around to returning to the mall. He said he'd take care of it himself. "But I took another look at this one and decided it was too funky to pass up. Plus, we match! Almost."

Now was not the time to dwell on the fact that sea foam and powder blue are a total mismatch. We were the Clash, and not in a cool way.

"So are you nervous?" he asked.

"I'm keeping a brown paper bag in my clutch in case I feel the sudden need to vomit. What does that tell you?"

Keith rubbed my shoulders. It occurred to me that this was the first time we'd touched since the car accident. "Do you want to practice your acceptance speech on me?"

"As jinxes go, I think that's probably the jinxiest."

"Suit yourself. I just thought you might like someone to bounce ideas off of. Have you got one written or are you going to wing it?"

I saw my earrings on the side table—a good reason to wriggle from his touch. "You act like it's a sure thing."

"That's because you act like you can't win."

"I just don't want to act like we *ought* to win. My mom's done that her whole life. And look at what that's gotten her."

"Fame, fortune, and an ungrateful daughter," Mom said, having heard just enough as she made her entrance at the top of the stairs. "What else could a star want?"

"An Emmy?" Keith asked, and not in a whisper, either.

Mom ignored Keith as she swanned down the steps, dripping diamonds. Gina was right behind her.

"Mallory, you look radiant," Gina said, genuinely thrilled for me. "Am I right or am I right?"

Mom looked me up and down, but the best she could muster was "Mmhm. All right, everyone, it's time to go."

Keith scowled. "We're all going *together*?"

"The network only sent one limo," I apologized.

"Feel free to walk," said Mom, "or even stay behind."

"But then I'd throw off the seating arrangement," said Keith, his jaw clenched.

"Oh, that's silly. The people who plan these ceremonies are ready for any contingency. They'll just move people around. I'm sure Dallas wouldn't mind sitting next to Mallory," said Mom, breathing frost.

Keith tensed. I stepped in. "Shall we? I think the driver's ready for us."

But Keith wasn't letting go. "Shouldn't we wait for *Richard*? Or has he made other arrangements?"

"I'm not worried about Richard," said Mom. "However, I do worry about you, Kasper, especially on that red carpet. Will you be able to behave yourself among all the paparazzi?"

"Gee, I really hope so, Ms. Hayden. How about if I make you a deal? If you help me keep my temper in check, I'll help you do the same. 'Cause all those reporters are bound to want to know more about how it feels to be twenty years closer to the grave than you were a week ago."

All of a sudden, getting into that limo with Mom and Keith seemed like getting into a death trap. I prayed to God we wouldn't hit traffic.

God was not on my side that day. The traffic on every freeway from Santa Barbara to Sunset Beach moved with all the urgency of a stoner to a drug test. Things were quiet at first, thanks to Gina's efforts to keep the peace. Whenever my mom asked how she looked, Gina would distract her with a crinkled brow, and *poof*, out came the hand mirror. Mom stopped asking after her third lipstick adjustment. There came a point when even she could find no wrong with her reflection.

"Relax, Mom," I said. "Nobody's going to call you out on the red carpet."

"It does help that the walking robin's egg on your arm is a lock for the top of all the worst-dressed lists," she sneered.

"Bring it on," said Keith, despite the squeezing I was giving his wrist. "I'll consider it a badge of honor."

"Way to think ahead, Krispin. I hope Mallory considers your street cred a fair trade for her good name. After all, every picture of you mugging for the camera in your Mod Squad uniform will be captioned with her name first: Mallory Hayden, seen here with date, sometime juvenile delinquent, Kieran So-and-so."

Keith let her statement hang in the air for a moment. "Anybody know what the Mod Squad is? Is that from, like, the fifties?"

Mom bit her lip hard, smearing her tooth with lipstick. Or was it blood? Gina tried to get her attention, but Keith's attitude was ringing in Mom's ears. "So these are the qualities you value in a boyfriend? Insolence? Superiority?"

"Can we all just not talk?" I pleaded, shielding my eyes. "Does anyone here want to have frown lines in their first picture on the red carpet?"

Keith looked at me sharply. "Before we do that, I'd

appreciate it if we heard more about the qualities you value in a boyfriend. Specifically, is there anything more to me besides insolence and superiority?"

I looked at Keith. Mom looked at me. Gina looked out the window.

"Of course there is," I said, hoping my telepathy would kick in and he'd hear me screaming *LEAVE IT ALONE.*

"How about if I get you rolling? I'm loyal."

Mom tsked. "And presumptuous."

Keith leaned forward. "Patient!"

"Egotistical!"

"Tolerant!"

"Infantile!"

"Feel free to chime in anytime, Mallory! At this point I'll take hot, or drives stick, or bathes!"

"Even a dog bathes," muttered Mom.

"Would you two listen to yourselves?" I said. "Amelia and I get along better than this!"

Keith flicked the intercom switch and told the driver to pull over.

"That'll be a minute, sir—we're at a standstill and I'm in the center lane."

"Forget it," Keith said. He opened the door and stepped out. I sat there in shock for two seconds, and Gina blurted, "What are you waiting for, Mallory?! Go get him!"

I hitched up my gown and scrambled into the shimmering LA heat. Keith had already stalked three car lengths down the median. Lying on the pavement was his bow tie, the one I told him he didn't have to wear, the one he wore anyway, just to make me happy.

"Keith, you're gonna get hit by a car. Come back!"

He spun around, his arms open wide. "Why should I? I can think of a million reasons not to get back in that car. Your Mom. Your cast. Your show. Your priorities. Can you give me one good reason why I should?"

"Come on, princess," belched a voice above me. A mutton-chopped big rigger leered down from his truck's cab. "Tell him you love him!"

Keith stood waiting.

"Because I want you to be there."

Keith stood waiting.

"Isn't that good enough?"

"How about if you tell me once more, with feeling this time?"

Muttonchops cleared his throat and ducked back inside. I could hear *Likely Story* playing from his portable TV.

Keith went on. "I just don't believe you, Mallory. And I don't think you believe you, either."

"Miss?" It was our chauffeur, calling me. "Traffic's clearing up ahead. You'll want to get back in."

I turned to Keith, blinking back tears. "Please get back in the car, Keith."

He shook his head. "I'm not Keith," he said. "I'm not Kal or Kanye or Kellan. And we're not George and Gracie or Nick and Nora or Sid and Nancy. I'm Erika. And you're me. And the show's you."

"Mallory," my mother yelled, window down. "Let's go!"

Keith's eyes glistened. "And your mom's still your mom."

I took a deep breath. Suddenly I felt like I'd been here before, and it hit me: episode eighty-eight. Ryan and Jacqueline confront each other as a mighty spring gale plucks shingles from her roof. This was Act VI-D. The end of the show. The cliff-hanger. The prelude to the slam bang of a May sweeps Friday. This was Jacqueline's big speech, raw and real and revealing. She made her case, and we tightened on Ryan to leave the audience wondering. . . . Would he stay? Or would he really turn around and walk away into the rain and night?

I'd written that speech. I knew it by heart. I knew it was a winner. It was on the tip of my tongue.

But that's where I left it. Those weren't my words anymore. I wasn't Jacqueline, and Keith wasn't Ryan. I could write their dialogue with ease but was unable to write my own.

"Go to the Emmys," Keith said. "Have a good time. Bring home the gold. I'll still root for you. But I'll be doing it from home." And he walked off, not looking back.

When I climbed into the limo, Mom had the television turned on and tuned to the red carpet arrivals.

"Where's Keith?" asked Gina.

I couldn't look at her. "We're good to go," I spoke into the intercom. The car sprang forward.

"Oh, honey . . ." Gina shook her head. "Look at you, you're a mess." She dug around in her purse, but the first person to offer me a tissue was my mother.

"Clean yourself up. We'll be there shortly."

I batted the tissue from her hand.

"What is the matter with you?!" she spat.

"Keith dumped me. You won."

Mom said nothing, preferring to feign interest in Tyra Banks's Emmy gown.

"Go on, Mom. This is your big moment. Give me your victory speech. You know you've been rehearsing it for months. Lay it on me."

"I haven't won anything, yet."

"I'm sorry you think so, because you're not going to win anything else tonight. I made sure of that."

"What is *that* supposed to mean?"

Savor this moment, Mallory. Forevermore you shall associate the intoxicating smell of Armor All with your mother's utter annihilation.

"It means I'm the one who leaked your birth certificate to LikelyWhorey."

"Excuse me?"

Gina covered her mouth. I wondered if she was going to scream or throw up.

"I broke into the safe, took out your birth certificate, scanned it, and passed it along to the fine folks at Likely-Whorey."

"You wouldn't—"

"What, out-scheme you? Meddle in your life, butt into your affairs, mess with your job, undermine your relationship with your boss, take away your fiancé? Need I go on?"

"No." She paused long enough to pour herself several swigs of something clear from the minibar and for me to realize I was holding my breath. "I don't need you to recount all the ways you think I've wronged you."

"Because they're your greatest hits, right? You know them by heart." I was frenzied, slicing away at her with the scorn I'd honed for years. But she just sat there and took it. Not a single counterattack for what I'd pulled. Not even a word to defend herself. She just sat there and took it. Naturally, I thought she'd been replaced with an evil twin.

"This is it?" I asked, so tired of it all, but having to go through it anyway. "I out your real age and all you can muster is a shrug?"

"Shall I open a vein?" she asked, licking her teeth clean of alcohol. "Would that satisfy you?"

"Why don't you start with an apology? We'll work up to the bloodletting."

She laughed bitterly.

"You put far too much stock in the power of words, Mallory. How writerly of you. But it takes a performance to give life to dialogue, and I'm just not a good enough actress to sell you on an apology I don't mean. I've done nothing to be sorry for. Unless making sacrifices for my daughter is something to be ashamed of, in which case I'm the sorriest woman alive."

I was stunned speechless. This was supposed to be my moment. This was supposed to be—

"I abandoned the show that made me a star—and why? For you and *Likely Story*. I accepted a role as a"—here she paused to brace herself—"*guidance counselor,* and a wardrobe that's fifty percent tweed, and I did it for you. Every interview I sit down for begins with the question 'How does it feel to take orders from your teenage daughter?' I smile and shake my head and give you the credit you're due. . . . It feels like it takes hours! But do I get the same consideration from you? Never. On the odd occasion you deign to speak to the press, it's always Dallas this and Francesca that. After a career spanning decades, I've been reduced to playing your cheerleader. If I'd known that being on your side was a sin worthy of betrayal, I'd have destroyed *Likely Story* before the network ever signed off on it. Don't think I couldn't have. But it's not in my nature to sabotage your dreams, Mallory. No matter what you think I may have done, I'd never stand in your way."

She was on some new medication. That had to be it. It had made her completely forget the past.

"You jumped ship on *Good As Gold* because it was dead last in the ratings and about to be canceled," I reminded her. "More people were watching a test of the Emergency Broadcasting System than Geneva's latest hysterical pregnancy. So don't tell me it was your blessing that got *Likely Story* off the ground. I've gotten more support from Richard, and that's saying a lot."

"Richard is not your friend," she said. "He'd write the show himself if he had his way. He's still intent on punishing Dallas for his insubordination when the show was just getting off the ground—he was planning to sell the network on a story in which Ryan starts a dogfighting ring. If I hadn't suggested a pairing with me, your muse would be spending the next six months of tape dates in a hospital set, recovering from an on-screen mauling, and you would be writing public-service announcements for PETA."

"I—I don't believe you," I stammered as I groped around in my purse. "Richard and I may butt heads, but he believes in me." I found what I was looking for and thrust it at her. "At least he wants me to succeed—and finds a way to say so."

Mom took one look at the worn piece of paper I held in my hand and tsked. It was the press release the network had put out after the nominations were announced . . . the one with the following passage underlined in red pen:

When asked to comment on Likely Story's accomplishment, Marilyn Kinsey of Soap Opera Summary said this: "Story. Plain and simple. Mallory Hayden is a fresh, courageous voice in the world of soaps. Her ideas are original and her characters are bold—and Real. She's bringing people back to daytime, and for once the Academy is rewarding fine work and not the same old drivel that we've all become accustomed to."

"You think Richard left this for you?" she asked. "He doesn't even know which room is yours. I slipped that under your door, not him."

I looked at the passage again, this time through a haze.

Mallory Hayden is a fresh, courageous voice in the world of soaps. Her ideas are original and her characters are bold—and Real.

"And what about me and Keith?" I persisted. "How does siccing LikelyWhorey on us translate to you having to make a sacrifice for me?"

"Do you think I would stoop so low as to conspire with anonymous cloggers?"

"I think you mean 'bloggers,'" said Gina.

"Whatever. I may have suggested the story in *People,* but I did so only after you made it clear you were longing for Dallas. You're the one who aligned yourself with those trolls on the computer, Mallory. Not me."

Cleaned out of ammo, I turned to the only buddy I had in this foxhole and begged for a reload. "Do you buy this?" I asked Gina.

"Leave her out of this," my mother said sharply. "Unless you want to force our friend to choose sides. In which case, I shouldn't be surprised. You've already thrown your own mother to the wolves. Why stop there?"

"God, I am sick to death of the both of you!" Gina suddenly cried. "You," she shot at Mom, "should know better than to play the long-suffering type in front of me. I know all your dirty little secrets. And you"—she turned to me—"can afford to give your mother the benefit of the doubt this once. She doesn't even have an e-mail address. You think she'd know the first thing about getting in touch with a couple of evil bloggers and giving them the lowdown on your love life?"

The outburst shut us up long enough for the red carpet arrival show to register in our ears once more. Joy Behar was interviewing Alexis. I wouldn't have paid any attention if I didn't then notice her date:

Jake . . .

"We met at my charity softball game," she gushed. "Jake's my fan club president's brother. She's around here somewhere."

Joy turned the conversation to LikelyWhorey.

"*Likely Story*'s been the talk of the red carpet this year, and not just because of all its nominations. There's been a lot of gossip buzzing around the Internet about your co-stars and head writer. Has it been distracting?"

"Mallory's a great girl," Alexis said with her trademark sad eyes. "I feel really awful for her. She gets a bad rap. Just this morning, there was something else on that ugly Web site." The picture cut to Keith's mug shot, beneath which ran a block of text. Joy narrated.

" 'Keith headed for juvie? Duno with Mallory?' "

"I'll never understand your generation's slang," said Mom. "What does *duno* mean?"

"It's *dunzo*. With a *z*," I said.

With a *z*.

My heart skipped a beat.

With a *z*.

Jake had his arm around Alexis. She was saying something, but I was too busy cataloging all of LikelyWhorey's entries in my head. . . .

"Oh God," I whispered.

The intercom crackled to life. "We're here," said the chauffeur. We pulled to a stop, and I suddenly noticed the din pressing against the limo.

"Mallory? What is it?" asked Gina.

"I know who's behind LikelyWhorey." How could I not have known?

Mom perked up. "Who?"

The chauffeur opened the door, and the roar battered us. Before us was the red carpet, a long, crimson tongue stretching all the way to the maw of the Kodak Theatre. And on it, right in front of us, was Joy Behar, a camera crew, and Alexis, Amelia, and Jake—LikelyWhorey's masterminds.

The cameraman swung in our direction. I heard Joy say, "And here they are now!" I locked eyes with Alexis first, and then Amelia.

Then I closed my fist. And lunged.

My mom's Emmy fate was now out of my hands.

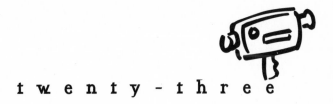

twenty-three

Two against one is not a fair fight. But I had four things working in my favor. One: the element of surprise. Two: blind rage. Three: the willingness to fight dirty. Four: the sound of Scooter egging me on from the spectator stands.

I reenacted Alexis's pillow fight with my mother—oh, she must have loved setting that one up—only this time I was the one doing the slinging, and I was using a purse full of MAC makeup and discarded speeches. Down she went. Amelia screamed bloody murder and bolted, forgetting she was dressed in floor-length silk and three-inch heels. She went down all on her own. Jake didn't know what to do: get out the smelling salts for Alexis or get in my way. He chose wisely.

I caught a fistful of Amelia's hair before she could crawl to the safety of the shocked crowd, and I pulled her to her feet, breaking one of my heels in the struggle. She was mine, but she was far from helpless. I had to make this count. Especially since I could see security bearing down on us from a Rosie O'Donnell–related altercation not far up-carpet. She keened as I dragged her past the cast of *Tropical Hospital* and right up to Joy Behar, to whom I offered my handshake.

"Nice to meet you, Joy. My name's Mallory Hayden. I write *Likely Story*. And this classy young lady is my ex–best friend, Amelia. She's got something to say to your audience. Go on, Amelia. Tell the nice lady how you and Alexis and Jake know all about what it's like to run LikelyWhorey."

The stream of swears that Amelia let loose later cost the network twenty million dollars in FCC fines. I told the network president, Stu Eisenhorn, to take it out of my salary.

I twisted my hand, and Amelia crumpled. "We don't have all day, Amelia," I said. Among the many heads bobbing for a better look were Gina's, Mom's, Javier's, Francesca's, Luc Franklin's, Marilyn Kinsey's . . . and Dallas's. I took a split second to worry that he'd lost all respect for me, and then I got over it. I'd lose all respect for myself if I didn't extract a confession from Amelia. "Spill it now. Or start investing in hats."

"Fine! Yes, we started LikelyWhorey! Happy now?!"

I let her go. And no, I wasn't happy.

"You act like it's something we should be ashamed of. I'm glad we did it! Somebody needed to teach you a lesson! And everything we said was true, wasn't it?"

The cameras were again turned on me, but the only gaze I felt was Dallas's.

"Deny it, Mallory. Tell us you aren't the kind of girl who steals another girl's boyfriend. You'd never choose your own success before your friends, right? And you're too good a person to string along your boyfriend while you figure out if the star of your show is into you. Tell us we're wrong."

I could push my way out of the cage of microphones

surrounding me, but my silence would speak louder than anything I said. Sixteen years of growing up in LA and watching my mother manipulate the media had trained me for this moment. I knew how to satisfy them and craft my image at the same time. With a single sound bite I could mute Amelia and render her a fool. No one would expect anything less. It would just be the latest salvo in a war we'd been fighting since I'd turned my back on her . . . the ever-widening conflict that had claimed victims not just of the two of us, but of Keith, Dallas, and my mom, too.

Any number of possible answers would have satisfied Joy Behar. But only one would satisfy me.

"I'm sorry I hurt you, Amelia."

She took a breath to retort, but stopped, unprepared for the blow I'd landed.

"I should've stuck by you. I made a bad decision. I was wrong. I wish I hadn't learned that lesson at your expense. And I hope you'll forgive me."

Now it was Amelia's turn under the spotlight, an opportunity she'd been seeking her whole life. She could either seize the moment or squander it. There was never really any doubt how she'd play it. She always folded under pressure.

"Forget it."

Joy turned to her camera. "You heard it here first, folks. Immaturity is alive and well in the American teenager." She nodded at me before adding, "But not all of them."

I didn't bother to correct her. I had miles of apologies and more news to make.

I stepped over a woozy Alexis and then lobbed my last grenade.

"And just for the record . . . I don't have a boyfriend anymore, thanks to you."

The throng of reporters exploded behind me. Dallas called out my name. I wanted to stop and tell him everything. I owed him, big—but I owed my mother more. So I made my way up the steps to the theater alone, stopping just once to survey the carnage I'd wrought. Jake was helping Alexis into a car. Amelia was gone, and my mother was mobbed by reporters, no doubt once again answering questions that were all about me.

But this time she was beaming. Truly beaming.

I was her girl, after all.

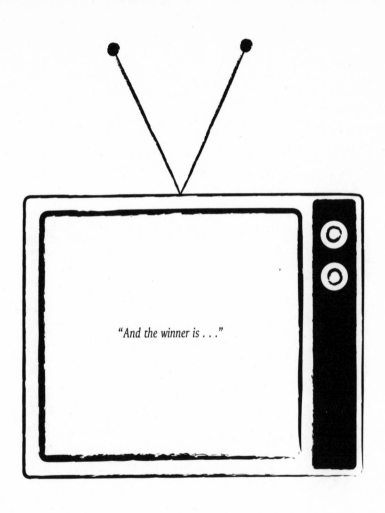

"And the winner is . . ."

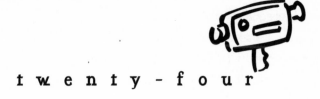

twenty-four

My newly acquired reputation for violence preceded me all the way to the ladies' restroom, which cleared out as soon as I hobbled in. I took it as a compliment.

The door swung open behind me, and Tamika came in. "I'm unarmed," she said, hoping for a smile.

"How'd you find me?" I asked.

"Easy. Everyone was running in the other direction. How's your smacking arm?"

"It hurts."

"I should think so. You know you practically broke Alexis's jaw, right? You look hot, by the way."

"Seriously?"

"Yes to both. Don't worry about it. She'll be thanking you when she loses ten pounds on a liquid diet. And we get to turn Sarah mute!"

"What have I done?" I asked my reflection.

"Exactly what you and I and half the cast have wanted to do for months. Did you know there was a pool? The First Person to Slug Alexis pool. My money was on Francesca."

"How much did you lose?"

"Let's just say it'll be another six months before I get my new Mercedes."

Now I was smiling. But just a little.

"It's not just Alexis," I said, sniffling.

"I know," Tamika said, squeezing my hand. "It's the talk of Hollywood and Highland. What can I do to help? Name it."

"Please stop being so nice to me. I don't deserve it."

Tamika squeezed my hand tighter. "I know you don't. You were supposed to return the compliment and tell me how I'm rocking this dress, but you know what? It's Emmy day. And everyone gets a clean slate on Emmy day. Besides, you're not only my friend, you're my boss, and I need this job."

I squeezed back. "I can't fire you. You keep me sane. And nobody writes Vienna like you do."

"That's more like it. Keep that praise coming and I'll have your back forever," she said. The voice of the telecast's director boomed over the loudspeaker in the lobby outside. *"Please take your seats, the ceremony is about to begin."*

"Do you think you're ready to face your public?" Tamika asked.

I shrugged. "I don't care what they say about me. Let me ask you something, though. Where do you think they keep the envelopes with the winners?"

"Why?" she asked, alerted.

"I wonder how hard it would be to switch one of them out."

She rolled her eyes and pulled me toward the door. "I'm going to pretend I didn't just hear that."

My only idea, shot down. My mom's Emmy fate was now out of my hands.

I entered the theater right before the show went live. The cast of *Tropical Hospital* pointed and whispered as I did my perp walk down the aisle, shoes in hand. I caught the eye of Luc Franklin as I passed by.

"Hope you're ready to go home empty-handed, Hayden," he called.

"I'd rather go home empty-handed than go home with you, Luc."

I heard a few titters from the *All My Affairs* section.

"From what I hear about you, you're not going anywhere with anybody," he returned.

"Hey, Luc," said a voice. I looked down the aisle to see Dallas approaching fast. "How's your batting average these days?"

This was met with general snickering from casts and crews of the three shows seated in the area. Luc sank into his seat.

"May I show you to your seat?" Dallas asked.

I took his arm but averted my eyes for fear I'd melt.

"What happened to your shoes?" he asked.

"I broke a heel breaking Amelia's will to live. Small price to pay, really."

The director's voice sounded once more. *"Please take your seats, we are thirty seconds from air."*

Dallas delivered me front row center and leaned in close as I sat down, so close I could feel his breath warm my ear.

"Good luck," he whispered.

I shivered.

"You, too," I said. He started to walk away.

"Dallas!" I called to him. He turned to me. There were so many things to say. But all I could get out was "Have you got your speech?"

"I scrapped it," he said. "I decided I needed something that applied more to the situation at hand."

He walked to his seat across the aisle. "What a gentleman," said the woman next to me, an older lady in a spectacularly frilly gown. It was then that I realized she was in the seat reserved for Keith. "I'm a seat filler," she said, reading my mind. I told her to settle in for a long night.

Richard sat on the other side of me, and Mom next to him. If I hadn't known better, I'd have thought they were strangers to each other. As the lights dimmed and the generic canned Emmy music blared, I noticed that all of our nominees were positioned with unobstructed paths to the stage. Mom was perfectly positioned for a short trip to the center podium. *Maybe this is a good sign,* I thought.

Richard leaned over to me. "You know the show paid for Alexis's Emmy ticket, don't you?"

"I'll write you a check. Was it really your idea to turn Ryan into a dog abuser?"

Richard paled as the hosts walked out onstage to applause and introduction.

"He brought the soul patch to daytime television; she's roller derby's greatest star! Ladies and gentlemen, please welcome . . ."

We were under way.

———

Last year's winner of the Emmy for Best Younger Actress presented the award for this year's Best Younger Actor. She was Camilla Cortez, and had been so honored for her daring portrayal of a young girl who went through life color-blind. Imagine . . . never knowing the difference between a green apple . . . and a red delicious. . . .

I checked in with Dallas, who appeared to be making a meal of his fingernails. Next to him was Francesca, who exposed a flask she kept hidden in her purse and offered him a sip. Dallas shook his head violently and pushed it away, just as five roving cameramen appeared and took their places in front of each of the nominees.

". . . proved that not all leprechauns were lucky," Camilla continued. "Our final nominee spent the year trying to make it work with the girl he loved, only to discover that sometimes love just isn't enough. Here's Dallas Grant playing Ryan, the young hero of *Likely Story*."

The big screen above the stage lit up. Dallas and Francesca were on Jacqueline's front porch as the storm worsened, weighing down on them. It was the same scene I'd imagined reenacting with Keith just hours ago on the freeway. It didn't end well for anybody.

Jacqueline had just made her final pitch for her and Ryan to stay together, only to have him turn around and walk away.

                    JACQUELINE
            Ryan, forget about me—

                      RYAN
              Already done.

                      269

                    JACQUELINE
             Just stay! It's dangerous
                     out there.

                      RYAN
              My chances of getting hurt
               are worse here. (SEE
               JACQUELINE, RAVAGED) I
             changed for you, Jackie. But
              it was a mistake. I don't
              like who I became.

                    JACQUELINE
                    Don't go.

                      RYAN
             (IN TEARS) Don't you get it?
               I'm already gone.

The lights came up as I wondered if everything I'd ever written for *Likely Story* had been a reflection of something I'd experienced myself . . . or was rehearsing for. All this time, I thought of my characters as living their own lives inside my head, and I was the one who had to draw them out and put them on the screen. But was it my life they had been living? Had I been sending signals through them all along? Not just signals to Dallas or Keith or my mother, but signals to myself?

Camilla tore into the envelope. "And the winner is . . . Dallas Grant!"

Likely Story's theme music descended on the audience, but

I could hardly hear it above my own cheers. Dallas was sandwiched between Francesca and Javier in a bear hug, and then he spun toward the steps. He shook his head in disbelief at the golden statuette, then leaned toward the microphone.

"Wow. First, I can't get off this stage without telling my mom to please forget about med school. It's not gonna happen." He got a few laughs with this, most of them from me.

"There were other things I was going to say and a lot of people I was going to thank, but I can only think of one of them right now." He looked down at me. "She's the one who taught me to speak in code. I hope you know how important you are to me. I've tried to make you see that. But I've always done better with other people's words than with my own, so I just want to conclude this by quoting some of yours . . . and hopefully you remember the translation."

He swallowed and took a big breath.

"Mallory Hayden . . . I loathe you."

And there it was.

Right in front of me.

There it was.

Some people were confused.

"Did he just say *loathe*?" the seat filler next to me murmured.

"Yes," I told her.

He loathes me.

Which meant . . .

He loathes me not.

I wanted him to come back down the steps. I wanted to eject the seat filler and have him sit down next to me.

I wanted to say I loathed him, too.

But that's not how award shows work. Dallas did not come back down to his seat, or to me. He was escorted off the side of the stage, to go celebrate his win with enquiring reporters.

I looked over to Dallas's empty seat. Francesca and Javier were both watching me. Seeing how I was taking it.

They knew.

Everyone knew.

But really the only thing that mattered was that Dallas knew.

And I was starting to know, too.

A lot happened after Dallas was escorted offstage, little of it given much notice by me. The theme of the evening seemed to be "Which of These Things Is Not Like the Other?" Like the hosts, there was an incongruous pair of presenters for every award doled out: undersea explorer/Playboy bunny; lion tamer/gourmet chef; ex–NFL star/rhythmic gymnast. A ventriloquist from public television did a bit with a puppet, though I later learned I'd confused the puppet with Barbara Walters. (In my defense, it could be very hard to tell with Barbara.) There was a song-and-dance medley, too: "Daytime Stars Salute Branson, Missouri!" And between all of this, commercial breaks, during which everyone got up and milled around or gossiped or stepped behind curtains to commit lewd acts.

I barely saw any of it.

I was busy replaying in my head the moment Dallas stood above me on the stage, announcing to the world that he loathed me. And if I wasn't seeing Dallas, I was imagining Keith hitching his way back to Tarzana, the half of my heart he'd taken with him squashed in his pocket.

But mostly I was wondering when Dallas would emerge from the labyrinth of press pens, gifting suites, and greenrooms the Emmy handlers were no doubt parading him through. It would be soon. And then the long wait would be over. He'd expect a response. And I'd have to give it to him. It was Emmy day for some and D-day for others. For me it was both.

For Mom it was all that and Memorial Day, too. Or so I realized when she glided onstage to much fanfare and introduced a *Good As Gold* retrospective. I hadn't even noticed her get up from her seat. Her appearance rated a solid ovation, instigated by none other than Richard.

I stared at her during the applause. And for once, I was seeing all these genuine emotions flash across her face—elation at being recognized, fear of being forgotten, comfort because part of her knew she belonged up there, and anxiety because the other part of her felt she wasn't good enough, and that even though she loved daytime—no one could argue with that—she never entirely knew whether daytime loved her back.

When the applause quieted, Mom looked to the teleprompter and began her scripted introduction.

"For forty years, *Good As Gold* was the standard-bearer for high drama, grand adventure, and big romance in daytime television. Viewers lived and died by what mysterious artifacts the Colonel would unearth in his mine; wept at the travails of poor beleaguered Hester and her trusty Saint Bernard, François; and thrilled to the exploits of my character, Geneva—sometime mayor, occasional fashion magazine editor, full-time dame. But all 'good' things must come to an end. And so this year we bid farewell to the cast and town that will always stay 'gold.' "

That should have been it. But my mother, as always, couldn't stick to the script.

"When you're old as I am," she began—and that one line got her even louder applause than before, nearly a standing ovation. Because this is what people wanted from my mother—a head-on collision, a brave reckoning. She smiled, then started over again.

"When you're as old as I am, you have seen all of the changes that have happened to daytime. You might wonder if we still have a place in this world. Well, I'm here to tell you—we *do* still have stories to tell. We *do* still matter in the lives of our viewers. We give them that essential daily dose of make-believe . . . and you know what it does? It makes them believe. Over and over. It makes them *believe.*"

The big screen lit up once more, and *Good As Gold*'s theme music, a jangle of country western and Copland-inspired strings, filled the theater. We saw the iconic image, *Good As Gold*'s slowly rotating safe, filled with gold bars and shimmering jewelry. As the longtime star, Mom was heavily featured in the montage. I recognized several clips from Geneva's iconic search for Shangri-la and the story that brought Mom closest to Emmy recognition, her daughter Diamond's courageous battle with rabies. With the fits and foaming at the mouth that Mom brought to the table, it might have appeared to the casual observer that the bat had attacked Geneva, not Diamond.

When the reel concluded, there was another round of applause. Mom returned to her seat, and the next presenter stepped into her place, announcing the nominees for Best Leading Actress.

I stole a look in Mom's direction. Richard had her hand in his. He'd moved out of the house, had barely said two words to her outside of work, but was still able to make some show of affection. Had I missed something? Had one apologized to the other right next to me without my hearing it? Was it an unspoken understanding that they'd had their fight and gotten over it? Was I wrong about them? Did they really loathe each other, too, in spite of everything? Or was it all for show?

The answers to these questions were vital. Somehow, the truth about my mom's relationship with Richard held the keys to my future with Dallas . . . or Keith. Or neither. All of a sudden I felt an incredible yearning to ask my mother for her advice . . . something I hadn't done since I needed to know the best color Crayola for Princess Ariel's hair.

"Isn't it obvious?" she'd answered before leaving for a date with a local news anchor.

It was too late to ask her for anything now. If she lost this award, it would be my fault. And if she won it, it would be in spite of me. I was on my own, and she was with Richard.

". . . Hayden's seasoned portrayal of a guidance counselor on the edge, and perhaps in need of a little guidance herself. Here she is in *Likely Story!*"

VIENNA

(WEARY) I'm tired of this
job, Principal Fine. I'm
tired of being shrugged at by
students. I'm tired of trying
to motivate them to take
their future in their hands
when they can't see beyond
the next weekend.

FINE

You're tired because you
care. You won't stop caring
if you quit.

VIENNA

(TREMBLING) Then fire me. If I
care any more than I do now,
I'll never get out of this
place.

FINE

Would that be so bad? (ON
VIENNA, FADE)

The big screen dissolved to a shot of the presenter, sur-
rounded by live images of each of the four nominees perched
in their seats, awaiting judgment.

I was stunned. I had no idea Mom had submitted material

so low-key. Her performance was subtle. There was none of the hand-wringing or scenery gorging that was typical of Emmy submissions. And I'd made sure she'd had scenes of just that variety last year, had been instructed to write her "an Emmy show." But she'd chosen something else altogether, and I could see the thinking behind it. Every year in the past, she'd submitted the same tape of weeping/railing/blaspheming/accusing/screeching that every other actress submitted, and every year she'd come up wanting.

So this year she'd used something real.

I turned to her then. I wanted to put my hand on top of hers and Richard's. Like a family would do.

"And the winner is . . ."

The presenter fumbled with the envelope.

Mom drew a deep breath.

"Anastasia Driscoll!"

There was a slight tremor in Mom as her body made an instinctive move to get up. It assumed she was going to win. And then she blinked. She mastered the impulse to take the stage. She stayed in her seat and did as she'd long trained herself to do in this moment, just in case. She set her face to a tight smile, stared straight ahead, removed her hand from Richard's, and applauded.

Anastasia's self-assured speech made no mention of the pressure she, Westerly, and Georgina had brought to exclude my mother from the running. But she did acknowledge the honor it was to have been nominated alongside two powerful performances.

Just two.

The camera still on her, my mother smiled graciously.

Every actress has her defenses.

And my mother was using them all right now.

Mom said nothing as the hosts returned to present the award for Best Writing Team. Richard tried to engage her. I don't know what he whispered in her ear, but it wasn't enough to even warrant her full attention. Tunnel vision was the only thing keeping her together at the moment. I tried to get her attention, tried to tell her I was sorry. But she kept looking straight ahead.

Her heart, I thought, was broken.

I heard my name read aloud in tandem with *Likely Story* as one of the nominees. Up until this point, I'd genuinely forgotten I stood a chance at winning anything. But as soon as I remembered, it all came rushing back. How ugly the Emmy-loss hangover was. How it sent my mother into a depression every year. How I'd never been interested in the Emmys in the first place. How I'd somehow got caught up in the race and somehow become my mother in the process.

Suddenly there was a roar. Every mouth in the theater opened simultaneously and let loose a cheer that could have shaken the walls. Everyone was on their feet. Even Richard. I was the only one left sitting. Richard took my hand and pulled me to my feet. I had no idea what was happening, had zoned out completely, couldn't make sense of what Richard was saying until he pointed my gaze in the direction of the screen.

We'd won.

"Go!" Richard nudged me toward the steps to the stage, where Tamika and Ronald and Anna were waiting with the rest of the team, bouncing up and down, high on Emmy. I stumbled on my way up the steps, and as I regained my footing, I realized this one little trip would be forever available on YouTube. When I arrived at the top of the steps, a silky young model handed me the Emmy. It was heavier than I'd imagined. And shinier. I could feel its seductive siren power in my hands; it sang strong.

The standing ovation lasted until I reached the microphone. I looked across the room, the ceiling vaulted so high and the balcony expanding so far back that I understood the totemic power this moment held for actors. Standing there, before so many people, it almost felt like I had the world's ear.

I didn't know what I was going to say. I couldn't remember the network excutives' names from meeting to meeting—how was I supposed to do it live on camera? The applause died down, and I stepped toward the microphone, poised to speak. That's when I saw it: The last person standing was my mother.

And she looked proud. Very proud.

Maybe it was acting.

But I didn't think it was.

And that's when I knew exactly what I had to say.

The thirty-second acceptance speech clock, visible over the cameras in front of me, began to tick.

"I want to thank the Academy for honoring the team of writers standing up here with me tonight. This is a team award," I began. "It's for all the people behind me, who work tirelessly to keep *Likely Story* true to the goal we set out for ourselves on day one: to write a different kind of soap opera. I think that when you honor us here tonight, you honor that vision." There was a smattering of applause.

Relish it, Mallory. . . . It might be the last you get.

"I'm glad they'll all get their own statues backstage; otherwise I couldn't give this one up." The applause gave way to murmuring. "Because I don't want this. I never did. I was made to believe it was important. That the recognition of my peers meant something. But after the display I've seen here tonight, I have to question your sanity. How anyone could award Anastasia Driscoll"—now there were gasps—"she of the alien shoplifting plot"—people were really paying attention—*"over my mother . . ."* Now the music was rolling, ten seconds ahead of schedule. "It's a crime against taste, and just goes to show you'll all be canceled in five years, but we'll still be here, I'll still be here, and my mother will still be here, sixty-five years of age and still acting circles around the rest of you dinosaurs!"

They cut off my microphone then. But I didn't care. I shouted my last line as loud as I could.

"This isn't my Emmy. It's yours, Mom!"

twenty-five

"Marilyn Kinsey wants a piece of you," Kimberly the Publicist warned me. After our rude dismissal, we'd been deposited backstage and into the hands of the network's handlers, which in this case meant Kimberly and Greg. Kimberly had informed me a few days before that the post-win press conference was normally a sedate affair. I'd been prepped for the usual array of questions: *Who are you wearing? How does it feel to win? What's next for Vienna/Ryan/Jacqueline?* But the pack of sheep had turned into a pack of wolves, and they were clearly out for blood. My blood, specifically. Word travels fast in Hollywood, especially when delivered live, on television, and in the form of a verbal bitch slap in the face of the industry.

Greg pulled me aside before we were thrust onto the dais. "Can I just say," he giddily whispered into my ear, "that you were before, are now, and always will be my hero?"

"Tell me again when this is all over," I responded. "Assuming you can put me back together again."

Marilyn Kinsey set the tone with her first question. "Where do you get off insulting all of daytime?"

It was downhill from there. Kimberly tried to keep things civil, but I didn't make her job easy. "You do it on a weekly basis with your column, Marilyn. I'm just trying to keep up."

Us Weekly and *People* were more interested in the beat down I'd administered on the red carpet. "Have you been informed whether Alexis and Amelia intend to press charges?" one reporter asked.

"On the advice of my lawyer—the one I've yet to hire—I'm going to have to decline comment on that subject."

"Where's Keith?" another reporter asked.

I paused for a second. "He decided not to come. Other than that, Keith is off-limits. Next question? Maybe someone would like to ask Tamika how she likes her new place in Santa Monica?"

"Do you and Dallas really have that bad a relationship? Why does he loathe you?"

Kimberly really knew her stuff, because she took that question as her cue to immediately wrap things up.

"Sorry to cut this short, but the award for Best Show is coming up and we need to get these guys back to their seats. Let's hear it for the Emmy-winning writers of *Likely Story*!"

Nobody clapped.

We didn't care.

Kimberly led us through the back halls of the Kodak and out into the main lobby for nominees and their guests, which was cordoned off, but not out of view of the general public. Our emergence rated a mixed bag of cheers and boos from among the ranks of the groundlings. I recognized a few of *Likely Story*'s fans from Alexis's softball game, and a sizable contingent of

Good As Gold fans, all of whom came to our defense when Anastasia's minions hissed.

I wrote a mental note to myself to never forget to thank the fans, even when taking a stand against Emmy injustice.

Kimberly shunted us off toward the entrance to the theater, but I stopped short. Sitting there cross-legged next to the double doors was Dallas, his Emmy in his lap. Our eyes met, and he scrambled to his feet.

"Go on without me," I murmured to Kimberly.

"But Best Show . . . ," she protested.

"We'll represent," Tamika promised her before bumping fists with me. "Ya done good, boss." Glancing at Dallas, who was slowly approaching, she added, "And I expect details at the after-party."

Then they were gone, and then it was just the two of us. And a horde of fans, cursing my name and begging Dallas to unbutton his top two buttons.

I tuned them out.

"Congratulations," Dallas said when he was close enough.

"You, too."

Something had changed. And we were still wearing the awkwardness of that change.

"Gold is your color," he said, nodding at the statue in my hand. "I guess this means I'm going to be shirtless all summer."

I didn't know what he was talking about. "Excuse me?" I said.

"Our bet?" he reminded me. "I guess I shouldn't have said anything."

Our bet. It seemed like years ago. A lifetime ago.

Everything was happening so fast.

"Don't worry about it," I said. "I thought we were just playing around. I wouldn't hold you to it."

"You can do whatever you want, but I have every intention of teaching you how to ride my motorcycle. A deal's a deal."

A lock of Dallas's hair swooped over his eyes, the way it always did whenever we stood close together and he looked down at me. And like always, I resisted the urge to brush it away. This time it was harder than ever. I wondered why I was still bothering to fight.

"So," he began, "have any thoughts on my speech?"

"It was brief," I said, closing what little gap there was left between us.

"Brief," he repeated. His hand touching my arm.

"I think you may have finally convinced your mom you made the right decision," I added, looking up at him, leaning in.

"I was referring more to the other part of the speech."

Leaning in.

"The part when you quoted me?"

Reaching up.

"Yeah. That part."

Brushing his hair from his eyes.

"What about it?"

Moving my hand over his ear, onto his neck.

"Do you have . . . anything to say about it?"

I hesitated for a moment as the music began to play from within the theater, seeping from the double doors. The nominees for Best Show were being announced. I was unfazed.

"There's not much to say, really. To paraphrase someone else, I put too much stock in the power of words. Sometimes it takes a performance instead."

And then, as *Likely Story*'s theme played on the heels of *Good As Gold*'s, I gave myself a boost, stepping my shoeless feet onto each of his, the better to kiss him the way I'd seen Francesca and Alexis kiss him countless times on screen, the way I'd secretly and not-so-secretly wanted to since the day I first laid eyes on him.

Lips close, then touching.

Lips touching, then pressing.

Lips pressing, then staying.

At last.

The nearby zoo of fans was on the verge of rioting, some rooting for us and some rooting against us. As we unpeeled, I nuzzled his neck and finished the thought that was continuously looping in my head.

"Dallas, I really, really loathe you."

He laughed and kissed me again, harder.

Kimberly burst from the theater. "Mallory, this is it! You need to— Oh."

Dallas and I broke apart, beaming.

"Put your shoes on and let's go."

"My heel's broken," I said with a laugh. All of a sudden there was no more drama, and the Emmy in my hand no longer felt as heavy. Especially when Dallas swept me up into his arms, lifting me like a bride.

"No worries, Kimberly," he said. "I know how to make an entrance."

Somebody shouted. "What about Keith, Mallory?"

And then another voice said, quieter and closer, "Yeah. What about Keith?"

Dallas swung us around—and there he was.

"Keith!" I gasped. "You came."

He looked shocked and angry and disappointed and floored, the Emmy ticket still dangling in his hand. "I figured I wasn't being fair to you. Silly me, huh?"

"Mallory!" screamed Kimberly, spinning from the door. "You won!"

The wave of applause wasn't as strong as when we'd won for writing, but it wasn't anything to shake a stick at, either.

"Mallory, we have to go," said Dallas, putting me down and touching my arm.

"We're talking here!" Keith yelled. I'd seen that look on him before. This was the one reserved for fender-bending paparazzi.

"No, *you're* talking. *We're* going," Dallas replied, offering me his hand.

I looked at Keith.

"I'm sorry," I said.

I took Dallas's hand.

At practically the same time, Keith drew back his arm and threw a punch, connecting with the bridge of Dallas's nose. Dallas stumbled into me, and I tumbled over, losing control of the Emmy I'd moments ago considered light as a cloud. As the winged muse careened end over end above me, I heard my mother's voice echoing over the microphone from the theater. *"I'd like to accept this award on behalf of my daughter. . . ."* Then the Emmy landed on my head with a clang. And I blacked out.

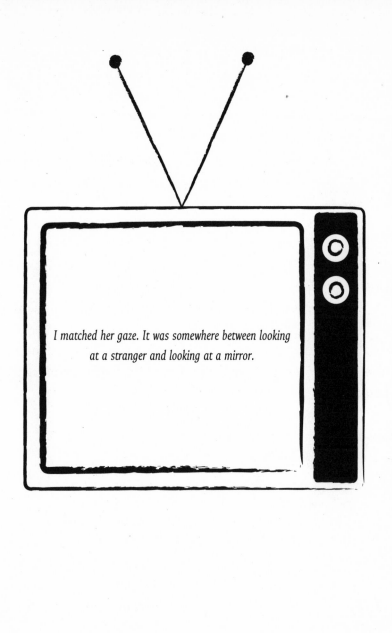

I matched her gaze. It was somewhere between looking at a stranger and looking at a mirror.

twenty-six

"Mallory?"

I woke up before I opened my eyes. The pain zipping back and forth across my head saw to that. A paper sheet crunched beneath me, and a hot light shone down from above. I pressed the back of my hand to my eyes.

"Mallory? How are you feeling?"

"Like I caught a harpoon to the head." I ventured an open eye. Keith sat beside me inside an otherwise empty ambulance. He sported a black eye and a blood-spattered shirt to offset his blue tuxedo.

"Do you want something for the pain?" He rummaged around in some drawers. Every clattering instrument was a sonic boom. "They've got Vicodin."

"It's okay," I said, sitting up. "I get the feeling I'm going to need my wits about me."

"The EMTs are outside, taking a look at Dallas. They want to check you out for a concussion but think you're fine. You want me to get them?"

"Keith. Relax."

We looked at each other for a moment. I nodded at his shirt. "Whose is that?"

"Dallas's," he said sheepishly. "I didn't know so much blood could come out of a guy's nose. They're saying he might need plastic surgery."

"At least he landed one in your eye."

"That was Tamika, actually. She came back out to drag you up onstage and saw what happened. Dallas was too busy looking after you to come after me, so she did the honors." He paused for a second, his shoulders drooping. "Dallas is a good guy."

"So are you," I said. "That was never the issue."

He looked to the floor of the ambulance. "I just wanted to make sure you were okay. And tell you I'm sorry I ruined the Emmys. You should have been on that stage tonight."

"I was. It's okay. I said everything I needed to say up there. There's still plenty I need to say to you."

"No need," Keith replied, looking back up at me. "I think we understand each other now."

This is what I wanted: another Mallory, one who I could send off with Keith. I knew she'd be happy. I knew he'd treat her well. But there wasn't any way to duplicate myself to get both of the things I wanted. There was only one of me, so I'd have to go with the thing I wanted more. Which was Dallas. Both Keith and I knew: It was Dallas.

I moved to stand up, and it was like the air was trying to push me back down.

"I'm a little shaky, still," I said. "Help me out?"

Keith held out his hand shyly. We'd been together off and on for over a year. But now that we were apart, the slightest touch felt off. He opened the doors in the back of the ambulance and we looked out at the Kodak. I turned to him.

"See you in school, Rick?"

"Absolutely, Ilsa."

He didn't miss a beat. I half expected the chopping *Casablanca* whir of airplane propellers and the foggy dreams of lives not lived to drown out the sad goodbye sounds. But they didn't. I heard—and felt—it all.

I found Richard, Greg, Kimberly, and Gina around the two EMTs, one of whom was wrapping Tamika's knuckles while the other, a little farther away, applied an ice pack to Dallas's face.

"There she is," said Tamika, alerting everyone to my consciousness.

"How's the head?" Richard asked. He held his Emmy like a baby. I hoped Tamika had gotten a picture.

"I can walk and talk, but the Emmy jolted my creative center. I may need a week at a spa on Maui to get it realigned," I told him.

"It'll have to wait. Stu called. The network's very pleased. They think ratings are going to skyrocket."

I looked him in the eye. "You know that's not the reason I did any of this, right?"

He nodded and actually grinned. "I know," he said. "And I like you all the more for it."

"I need to go check the other patient," I said.

"It's about time," Tamika chimed in. Gina and Greg nodded their agreement.

As I got closer, I could see that Dallas looked like a complete horror show. The EMT had just finished taping up his nose, and his tux looked like it had spent two seasons as an extra on *Grey's Anatomy.*

"Wow," I said. "You wear my damage well."

"I always knew you were trouble, Hayden," he replied. "Serious, wonderful trouble. The question is: Will you still loathe me when the bandages come off and I look like a building fell on my face?"

"Truth? I've always been a little intimidated by your beauty, Mr. Best Younger Actor. So this will probably just make me loathe you more."

Even under all the bandaging, I could see his smile. That, at least, hadn't changed.

"Any chance of getting that first lesson in tonight?" I asked.

"As long as you don't mind stopping at the ER on the way," he replied, tossing aside the ice pack.

"You're driving," I told him. The destination didn't matter. There would be a story wherever we went.

This was, I imagined, just the start.

And I could have left it there. I could have followed him into the nearest sunset. I could have taken his hand and walked past all the cheers and the boos, past all the reporters and photographers, right out of the Kodak Theatre and out of Hollywood and down to Mexico, where we could sail off into the future. But not yet. There was still one more thing I had to do.

"Have you seen my mother?" I asked. "Is she in the pressroom announcing to the world that I'm not really her daughter after all?"

I expected Dallas to make a joke, but instead, he just

pointed to a spot behind me. I turned and saw her there, leaning against the building, keeping an eye on all of us.

"I'll be back," I said.

"And I'll be here for you," Dallas promised.

I had to trust in that.

And, just then, I did.

I had no idea what she was going to say to me. Or what I was
going to say to her. I just knew it was time for something to
be said.

The lights from the ambulance were playing over us. Red—
blue—shadow. Red—blue—shadow.

I was ready for an attack. I was ready for a joke. I was ready
for her to say I'd ruined her night, or made her night. I was
ready for her to look at me like she didn't know who I was. I'd
seen all those things before.

But instead, she asked, "How are you feeling, really?"

"I'm okay," I told her. "I promise. Why are you over here?"

"I didn't want to get in the way. But I didn't want you out
of my sight, either."

Red—

blue—

shadow.

Red—

blue—

shadow.

"What's the last thing you remember?" she asked.

"Wondering why you were accepting the Emmy for Best
Show. And what you were going to say."

She regarded me with a cool stare.

"You can watch it later. I don't do second takes."

I leaned against the wall next to her. I was too tired to say anything back.

"Suffice it to say," she went on, "it wasn't as brilliantly worded as your speech. But it was just as heartfelt."

I sized her up. She was 5'6", 110 pounds, sixty years old, and faultless in appearance. She was also rigid, domineering, sarcastic, mean, inconstant, narcissistic, generally untrustworthy, and, let's face it, an alcoholic. But she'd given birth to me and midwifed my show. She was my mom. The only one I'd ever have. She was worse than most people conceived, but not as bad as I'd said. I had to take what I could get.

"I have your Emmy in the limousine," she told me.

"I told you already. It's yours." Any other daughter would have hugged her mother right then. I felt the impulse but held back, fearing she'd shrink away.

"Oh, I know. I meant your Emmy for Best Show. I'm not giving up the other one. I worked very hard for it. With difficult material, I might add."

"You wouldn't have me any other way," I said.

And while she didn't smile or pull me close, she did nod.

"You're right. I wouldn't have you any other way."

Red—

blue—

shadow.

Red—

blue—

shadow.

She reached out and put her hand under my chin, lifting it so I would look in her eyes. I'd seen her do this many times over the years—to her daughter Diamond on *Good As Gold*, to both Jacqueline and Sarah during their guidance sessions on *Likely Story*. But she'd never done it to me. Not once.

"I think it's time I told you about your father," she said.

I matched her gaze. It was somewhere between looking at a stranger and looking at a mirror.

"Yes," I told her. "I think it's about time."

About the Author(s)

David Van Etten splits himself between three minds and three bodies. They belong to:

David Levithan was Chris Van Etten's manservant and David Ozanich's tailor in his past lives. (How messed up is *that*?) In his present life, he writes teen novels.

David Ozanich writes about daytime drama for SOAPnet and ABC.com and writes travel essays for the Lonely Planet series, which recently published his first book. His "evil" alternate personality, Tex, has renounced his mafioso lifestyle to become a World Ambassador for Peace. His gatekeeper personality, Maxine, is an accomplished phone psychic, occasional dabbler in the black arts, and frequent fashion expert on *The View*.

In 1991, **Chris Van Etten** was diagnosed with a severe case of Soap Opera Rapid-Aging Syndrome. Overnight he grew from a gangly thirteen years of age to a still gangly but now self-assured thirty. He continues to draw on this character-building experience to this day, especially as a member of *One Life to Live*'s Emmy Award–winning team of writers.

To read more about David Van Etten, be sure to check out www.myspace.com/davidvanetten.